For Shiluta,

A Novel

Love in the Age of Coronavirus

Richard Gordon

Written at and during the pandemic to have a little intellectual satisfaction

the beginning

Cover and book design by Bob Salpeter

P.S. Some sexy scenes in this

Richd

This is a work of fiction.The names, characters, places, and incidents are the product of the author's imagination and are used fictitiously. Any resemblance to actual persons, living or dead, is entirely coincidental.

Dedicated to Alissa, Steven, and Jonathan

Love in the Age of Coronavirus

Chapter 1

"Shouldn't we wait until after the pandemic to fill out the census?"

Danny Miller laughed uproariously at seeing that line in an article on humor entitled "Don't Feel Guilty. It's OK to Laugh At Some of This." Assuring himself that there were more laughter-inducing jokes about the coronavirus crisis that he could chuckle at later, he turned to page one of the April 21, 2020 edition of the New York Times, glancing at one depressing article after another--increasing numbers of virus deaths in the U.S. and worldwide, no effective antidote or vaccine close to being developed until possibly early 2021, uncertainty about the antibody and swab tests, and no end in sight to the lockdown situation in New York City. The only sense of semi-relief that he and many others experienced was the daily Covid19 briefing of his new political hero, Governor Cuomo, who affirmed that upstate New York will be partially 'opened' some time soon, but New York City with its immense population density would remain closed.

Danny read articles in the paper about financial skulduggery at the highest and lowest levels of the U.S. economy--big corporations grabbing large amounts of government money supposedly destined for bailing out financially challenged small businesses; sophisticated tech thieves preying upon desperately poor people to steal a few hundred dollars that would have been used to pay their rent and buy food for the next month or two. It would be naive, he thought, to believe that companies or individuals would act any differently in a period of crisis and scarcity than they acted in normal times of relative plenty.

Danny shook his head when he saw an article entitled "The rich are loading up on diamond bracelets during the virus crisis." He recalled the film "Wall Street" in which the protagonist proclaimed that 'Greed is Good', a principle that operated universally in the United States to produce the 1% class of super rich, around 450,000 of whom escaped ("scampered away," as Danny termed it) from New York City at the beginning of the pandemic to flee to their country homes in the Hamptons, Berkshires, or northern Connecticut, leaving the middle and lower classes at the bottom of the financial totem pole to work, languish, or, worst luck of all, to catch the virus in New York City, now ominously identified as the epicenter of the pandemic. Danny felt that there should be a moratorium on predatory financial behavior during the current virus crisis, but individual behavior, with the notable exceptions of doctors, nurses, and hospital and social workers ministering to the virus-ridden ill, displayed the same ugly features as always, starting at the highest levels of government.

And there perched U.S. President Donald Trump who, in Danny's mind, was concerned only with his personal image, his financial interests, and the stock market as the barometer of his political ratings. Trump had minimized, nay, ignored, the virus problem in December and January, when China announced the existence of a malevolent new contagion appearing in the city of Wuhan, which was quickly locked down to prevent people circulating and the virus from spreading. The virus then began its insidious path to other countries, including the U.S., but Trump, seeking to avoid bad publicity, continued to ignore the evidence that the pandemic was seeping, nay galloping into the U.S. in rapid fashion. So every action the president took and every statement he made related to two narrow personal objectives--(1) avoiding responsibility for the lax, inefficient national government response to the burgeoning virus and (2) appealing to his conservative, evangelical base for political gain in the November presidential election. Danny and everyone he knew (with one or two exceptions) was strongly Democratic in political outlook, aghast at the lies, corruption, and malevolent actions of the president and his Republican party allies, one of the worst being the incarceration of immigrant children in cages on the southern border with Mexico where they languished and suffered to this day.

Even though the loss of life due to the virus climbed rapidly to fifty, then seventy, and then over one hundred thousand deaths--far more than the American dead in the Vietnam War--the President and his sycophantic, robotic Vice President refused to acknowledge the severity of the problem, continuing to go to meetings without face masks because wearing them would supposedly undermine their alpha male images and confirm that there was a dangerous pandemic out there instead of a 'phony, fake illness' promulgated by Democrats seeking to tarnish the president.

Sipping his coffee and munching on corn flakes laced with strawberries, Danny glanced at the thin sports pages of the New York Times. He felt bereft. Here as everywhere else, there was abnormality--college basketball games suspended a day or two before the March Madness playoffs, followed by the cancellation of games in all the professional leagues--basketball, hockey, baseball--all called off. Poof...they just disappeared, with no sign of when they might return.

In the present lockdown situation, life was barren for a sports fan like Danny. The ESPN sports channels, desperate to keep their viewers, played and replayed games from recent and distant past eras. The multi-series Michael Jordan documentary was fun to watch at the beginning, because it showed the incredible skills of perhaps the best basketball player in history, but as it moved along to amazing scenes of basketball championships won by Jordan and the Chicago Bulls in thrilling fashion, the series became unbearably repetitive, and Danny couldn't be bothered to watch it any more. He cursed his bad luck with respect to his favorite baseball team, the New York Mets, because with major league baseball now canceled, how would he know if the doleful Mets would lift themselves from the long-standing muck of inadequacy to have a sparkling season and possibly even make the playoffs in 2020? Another bummer for sports-obsessed American males, the professional football draft was being held the very next day, but with all the customary hoopla eliminated. The actual draft would be done remotely, with the players selected appearing in their individual homes either smiling broadly if they were selected at a high level or frowning sadly if chosen below their delusional expectations. Big bucks were at stake here, but the entire process seemed similar in Danny's mind to having sex remotely without physical contact.

Daniel had been a decent athlete in his youth. In high school he played a sport every season--soccer in the fall, basketball in winter, and tennis in the spring. In college at Tufts, he played freshman basketball and tennis, but didn't make the varsity in these two sports which he then played intramurally. He still played in pick-up basketball games in Riverside Park on weekends, as well as tennis in a fancy indoor tennis club with a partner twice a week. For Danny, how much better quality of life could he have in being able to play tennis indoors during snow storms in the winter months? However, the tennis club had closed in March, and indoor tennis was now history, as was outdoor basketball, given the fact that the city had removed the rims from the tall poles in the park to avoid social crowding. Danny was now limited to indoor exercise in the cold weather, riding his stationary bike for 45 minutes, doing 80-120 push-ups, and lifting weights. However, in good weather he made the trek to Riverside park to do a run or a long, fast walk.

Now with the lockdown, compelled to work from home, sitting at his computer for endless hours, he began to get 'cabin fever' (restlessness and utter boredom). So he instituted a mandatory policy of doing some form of exercise each day in the hope that it would be good both for his body and his mind. It definitely helped, and it got him outdoors almost every day. When he ran or fast-walked in Riverside Park, he would begin at 78th Street near his apartment and head up to the Columbia University neighborhood at 116th Street, sometimes going to the area beyond West 125th Street where a number of new Columbia University buildings were being erected, including a new business school to which Danny, an alumnus of the Columbia Business School on the main campus, had made a substantial contribution over a year ago. As a result, he was invited to attend special donor gatherings which furthered his aim of making contacts with wealthy alumni in connection with his new start-up company.

On his run Danny often stopped to look in the window at Smokey's at 126th Street, one of his favorite rib and beer places, now closed and delivering food only within a range of thirty blocks, excluding Danny geographically from deliveries to his apartment down on West 77th Street. Occasionally he bought some delicious smoked ribs, brisket, or pulled pork sandwiches to munch on at lunch or at dinner. Danny considered himself lucky to be in a culinary mecca zone of great food stores like Fairway, Citarella, and Zabar's, all close by on Broadway. He either bought prepared food for his lunches and dinners or ordered in from nearby Indian, Thai, Italian, French, and Israeli restaurants. Lately he had been trying his hand at cooking simple dishes like hot dogs, burgers, scrambled eggs, pastas, and steamed vegetables. A woman friend gave him her recipe for making shrimp scampi with pasta which he promised to make for himself the following week, but never did. Danny was far from starving in the present lockdown situation; in fact, the opposite was true. He found himself obsessing about food, eating more than normal, and he kept vowing to go on a diet, but that hadn't materialized yet.

Danny and his older brother Joel had grown up in West Hartford, Connecticut. His parents were of different religious backgrounds, his father a lapsed Catholic and his mother a lapsed Jew. Believing in the notion of free choice and not wanting to impose their non religious views on their sons, they took the boys to a Catholic Church on Christmas and Easter and to a conservative synagogue on Rosh Hashanah, Yom Kippur, and Passover. When the boys were considered old enough (Joel was five years older than Danny), their parents subjected them to religious and philosophical discussions at the dinner table. Their parents allowed each of them to choose to go to a church or synagogue, study on their own, wait until college to take courses on religion, or simply ignore the issue. Joel had been fine with the minimalist approach to religion, but Danny had many Jewish friends in the neighborhood and at school, and he pleaded with his parents to allow him to have a Bar Mitzvah. They reluctantly agreed, and at age ten, he went to Hebrew School four afternoons a week. However, this rigorous schedule interfered with playing after school sports and seeing his friends, and so a tutor was hired to instruct him in the essential elements of a Bar Mitzvah. She was small and hunchbacked (Danny referred to her as "The Toad"), but her Hebrew instruction was excellent, and she patiently guided him to perform his Haftorah in Hebrew and English and to prepare his speech on the importance of tolerance and acceptance of other faiths and non-faiths.

After the service, there was a noisy, festive luncheon party with his friends and relatives. His parents asked Danny if he wished to go to the synagogue Sunday school, but he declined. In fact, not long after his Bar Mitzvah, he abandoned Judaism, becoming successively an agnostic, an atheist, and a 'semi-Buddhist'.

A year ago, a friend recommended a spiritual philosophy called Metapsychiatry which combined spirituality and psychology. Its founder and progenitor was Dr. Thomas Hora, a Hungarian-American psychiatrist whose magnum opus was called "Beyond the Dream" which Danny had devoured in one reading and was now rereading. Before the pandemic, he attended lectures and group meetings run by disciples of Dr. Hora who had passed away in the 1990s, but these were now suspended because of the coronavirus. Still intrigued spiritually and intellectually by metapsychiatry, he continued to read Dr. Hora's works and meditate a few times a week.

His close friend Adam tried to drag a reluctant Danny to his synagogue on Friday nights, calling Danny a "post-Jew," someone who had been Jewish but had moved on to something else. Danny didn't dispute the description, but he retorted that Adam might be culturally Jewish, but, as he had admitted, didn't believe in God, while he, Danny, believed in God, thanks to Metapsychiatry, but didn't feel culturally Jewish or linked to any of the major religions for that matter. The two guys would tease each other mercilessly over this subject, with neither of them budging an inch in his belief or non-belief.

Danny's girl friends had been of different creeds--Jewish, Christian, and Asian. Over the years, he happily accompanied his Jewish girl friends to synagogue on the High Holy Days, as well as to Passover Seders; his Christian ones to church on Christmas and Easter; and his delightful Korean girlfriend of a few years ago to a Buddhist temple in Woodstock.

At the moment Danny defined himself as being 'between girl friends'. At age thirty-two, he still felt reasonably young, but lately in his lockdown condition, he began to feel lonely every so often, and he missed not having a woman to be with. Lately he had even begun to contemplate the notion of marriage and fatherhood which he fantasized could happen in the next year or two after the present lockdown ended. However, in order to marry and have children, he would need a compatible (nay, perfect) woman who was attractive, intelligent, good-humored, willing to have children, and easy to be with. The entire package, immensely difficult to find in normal times, was impossible now in the covid era.

Danny thought a lot about his older brother Joel who had married in his mid twenties and was now the proud father of a boy, Andrew, and a girl, Anya, eight and six years old respectively. Danny loved playing the doting uncle, going as often as he could to South Nyack by car or by train to Tarrytown and bus across the Tappan Zee Bridge to hang out with his niece and nephew. In good weather he took them to a nearby park with a soccer ball, basketball, baseball and gloves, and a small football in order to teach them the rudiments of these sports, while having immense fun in the process. He also paid for tennis lessons for Andrew and Anya indoors in the winter and outdoors the rest of the year. The kids loved seeing him, badgering him on phone calls to come to Nyack to play sports with them right away. He went as often as he could before the virus struck, but that seemed impossible now. He asked Joel if he could come anyway, but Joel, citing the many cases of coronavirus in New York City (still called the 'epicenter' of the virus in the U.S), reluctantly begged him to wait until the pandemic ebbed.

Danny's urge to consider marriage and have a child or two was a new phenomenon, since until very recently he loved being single and had scorned the idea of getting married. He had passed up a good opportunity a couple of years earlier, when a friend fixed him up with an attractive, interesting woman named Joan. After seeing each other for almost a year, she put pressure on him to consider marriage, but he declined, saying that he wanted to keep their relationship going in its present form, but not 'tie the knot'. Joan warned him that unless he changed his mind in the near future, she would move on. She did, and a year later sent him an email to announce her engagement, kindly wishing him 'similar luck' in finding the right person.

Danny continued to meet women through friends, work contacts, and dating sites. He connected pretty easily with women, often ending up in bed by the third or fourth date. However, no one had rocked his socks since Joan, and while he still 'dated', he was happy to spend much of his non-work time with his male and female friends, as well as keeping fit by doing Road Runner races in Central Park, playing basketball and tennis, and lifting weights at the nearby West Side Y.

Having majored in economics at Tufts University and then getting an MBA at Columbia, he had worked for seven years at two different corporations in business development and financial investment, making excellent salaries and acquiring stock options in the second firm which he was allowed to cash in progressively after he left by agreeing to train his replacement and undertake some short-term consultancies for the firm. Danny had invested his money wisely in the stock market, mainly in conservative companies with good dividends, but also in two high flying biotech firms, one of which recently got FDA approval for developing a new cancer-related drug which they began marketing widely. Soon Danny was worth over a million dollars. This enabled him to join with a friend from West Hartford and another from the Columbia 'B' School to form a start-up business which they had planned for over a year and then launched six months ago.

The company, called Allegria Inc. (Spanish for 'happiness'), focussed on 'bluetooth' technology, interfacing computer and cell phone communication and developing innovative software programs for the burgeoning older population, many of whom were not only baffled by the new social media platforms and computer technology, but also physically impaired (deaf, poor eye sight, immobile, etc.) Allegria created phone and computer "events" to assist the elderly and the impaired to communicate more easily with their families and friends on the computer, as well as to access news and stream entertainment programs (Netflix, Amazon, Hulu, and YouTube). He and his two partners had each invested $250,000 in the company, using the funds to rent an office on lower Fifth Avenue and hire two full-time employees, one in sales and the other in public relations. The three principal figures traveled around the country seeking contracts with companies such as IBM, Dell Computers, Google, hospital conglomerates, state pension bureaux, school systems with large pension funds, and local governmental agencies. The company was moving forward reasonably well, with trips planned to Europe and South America to scout out new potential clients. However, with the onset of the coronavirus two months ago, everyone in the company had to work at home, with travel in search of new clients or to service existing ones suspended.

Every other day at 10 a.m., the three principal officers, as well as the public relations and sales employees, engaged in a Zoom conference meeting. Danny, who had founded the company, was the nominal president of Allegria, with Steven and Jonathan each having the title of executive vice-president. When Steven learned that the term 'bluetooth' came from a medieval Danish king named Harald Bluetooth, who compelled the non Christians in ancient Denmark to convert to Christianity and in the process united his kingdom, the three guys invented medieval names for themselves and began to use this historical reference in their logo and in their advertising and marketing material for the company. Each of their cards had a picture of King Harald looking fierce.

Danny and his partners worried that a prolonged period of the virus lockdown could have a strong negative effect on their company, especially in the search for new customers in the U.S. and abroad. Every day he read about the closing of restaurants, theaters, movie houses, and small businesses like their own, as well as the gigantic number of lay-offs throughout the country, creating over thirty million newly unemployed in a matter of weeks. The federal government was borrowing or creating new money in the billions (maybe trillions) to alleviate the devastating economic situation, but recently the scandalous news came out that loans to small businesses were cast aside in favor of loans or grants to large affluent companies like Shake Shack and the Los Angeles Lakers basketball team, both hardly in need of financial bailouts.

Nevertheless, Danny and his team filled out a complex application for a loan of $500,000, a process that took them almost a week to understand, complete, and submit. No word had come to them from the federal government agency dealing with loans to small businesses, and Danny was not hopeful. He and his partners negotiated a reduction in the monthly rent for their office (which was not being used during the lockdown) and continued to pay salaries to their two major employees and the two secretaries at 80%

and to themselves at 50%. Danny, initially optimistic about the prospect of a business loan, became much less so and began to envisage drastically reducing or even eliminating the salaries of the three officers at some point in the summer. On an optimistic note, Danny continued to exchange messages and ideas with a company on the West Coast about a possible merger with or buyout of Allegria. Talk was cheap, though, and little progress was made, but the three partners agreed to continue discussions while avoiding any decision-making for the time being.

Every morning Danny read the liberal NY Times and conservative NY Post to follow the mostly awful news about the virus and about national politics. Danny watched the daily news briefings with Dr. Fauci, the eminent public health scientist whom Donald Trump could not completely ignore in the face of scientific evidence about the spreading virus. Trump, who had downplayed the pandemic problem initially and then did little or nothing to confront it effectively, ultimately closed down the Fauci news briefings which had made the president look like a fool. Ignoring scientific evidence and seeming to care only about his image, the stock market, and his reelection as president, Trump had displayed no concern for the national interest apart from his personal interest. In his interactions with foreign leaders, mainly dictators (China, Russia,Turkey, etc.), he blatantly asked for help in getting reelected in November 2020. He survived the impeachment hearings which centered around his quid pro quo offer to the new Ukrainian leader to investigate so-called financial shenanigans of Joe Biden's son in return for receiving advanced weaponry. Continuing to deny any responsibility for the pandemic, he proposed bizarre measures such as drinking bleach, while blaming Democrats and the liberal media for exaggerating the problem. Trump and Vice-President Pence refused to wear masks, even after some people on the White House staff came down with the virus. Wearing a mask every time he went outside, Danny felt that this purposeful neglect was a pitiful display of macho behavior whose purpose was to curry favor with the ultra nationalistic gun-toting male population that comprised much of Trump's political 'base' in the country.

He had little faith that Trump and the intimidated, craven Republican Senators and Congressmen would do much, if anything, for the snowballing numbers of the starving poor or for small businesses, since the president and the far-right Republican Senators were interested only in pandering to large corporations who would then repay them by donating large sums of money to Trump and the Republican Party in connection with the November election, unless the unpredictable, power hungry president tried to postpone or even cancel it. Seeking to avoid responsibility or blame for the expanding Covid-19 disease, Trump had begun to denounce the Chinese for originating and spreading the so-called 'China virus'. This was another blatant lie, since the virus on the east coast had come primarily from Italy. China dismissed any American critiques as "insane lies" and showed good will by sending masks and other medical equipment to the United States. Even after a total of over one hundred thousand deaths attributable to the coronavirus,Trump advocated the 'opening' of society, particularly in states where virus deaths were not abundant, because he was desparate to get the economy moving again, a crucial and necessary element in his strategy for reelection.

New York continued to have a huge number of both virus cases and deaths, and while Governor Cuomo made noises about the reopening of rural areas in northern New York State, no accurate prediction could be made about reopening the major cities, including New York City. If the present situation lingered until the fall, Danny wondered how on earth an election could be held when people were afraid of standing closer than six feet apart from each other.

Danny could well understand that people out of work, unable to put food on the table for their families, many bored and/or depressed, would champ at the bit to reopen society, since they would now be able to resume work and seek to recreate a 'normal' life. This was happening in many states where the virus numbers were low, but there was unfortunately a resurgence of virus cases especially in the South, Southwest, and California, as well as in more isolated places like Minnesota and Montana. Most of these places had 'reopened', with many so-called macho men and women shunning mask wearing and not practicing social distancing. Danny worried about his cousins in Tucson and in Austin, but he felt physically and psychically impotent to help them. He understood that there was very little that a single individual could do to alleviate the pandemic situation. He contributed money to charities feeding the homeless and the poor, but he knew that his modest cash contributions didn't amount to 'a hill of beans', as Humphrey Bogart put it so graphically to Ingrid Bergman in "Casablanca," one of his all-time favorite films.

So what was there to do or to read that could lift his spirits? He turned back to the article about humor in the age of the virus and read the lines "Jesus conducting the Last Supper by Zoom ("Judas, you on'") and "Anyone else starting to get a tan from the light in your refrigerator?" Not as funny as the census line, but welcome black humor to elicit a smile or two. He saw a weak joke about toilet paper hoarders. Then there was the definition of "your quarantine alcoholic name--your first name followed by your last name." Later in the day he would send these jokes to friends in California, Michigan, and Texas who weren't reading the Times and were therefore unlikely to find anything humorous about the virus.

In forty minutes it would be noon, the moment when he would put on his track suit and running shoes in preparation for his departure to nearby Riverside Park to do a long, lazy jog. He ran/jogged on Mondays, Wednesdays, and Fridays, while pedaling on his stationary bike and lifting weights in his apartment on Tuesdays, Thursdays, and Saturdays. Sundays he took off from doing any exercise, but he found that he was more restless that day than on any of the other day of the week, and he might have to alter his vow to take a day off from exercising. His life now was extremely structured, with his work, his exercise, and staying in contact with his family and friends. While admittedly repetitious and mildly boring, his schedule was at least keeping him physically healthy and mentally sane.

But there was the issue of sex or rather, the absence of it. Danny was used to regular sex with his girl friends. If he was in a fallow period, he could visit a Chinese/Korean massage parlor where he found accommodating young Asian women offering a 'happy ending' to him. Since he only went when he was very horny, he invariably asked for a 'happy beginning' which relieved his sexual tension right away and allowed him to lie on his stomach to receive a long, soft back massage. In the present lockdown period, he had no outlet for his sexual cravings, and so he began to masturbate (he used the less fancy term 'jerk-off') just to have an orgasm to relieve his sexual tension. Sometimes he watched a porn film to turn him on, but normally the fleshy women's bodies he saw on the screen didn't excite him. Always organized, he developed a plan to masturbate twice a week, on Saturdays and Wednesdays, and he found that he was thinking about it the day before, and this might induce him to go for it a day early. He laughed at Bill Maher's plaintive declaration on his recent Friday night TV show that he was tired of the same hands on his you-know-what and would welcome some new feminine hands. Pleasing himself was fine, but it was hardly a replacement for holding a woman in his arms.

Danny had a woman in mind to hold, someone he didn't know, but had recently begun to fantasize about. The problem was how to meet her, not an easy task in this period of enforced isolation. The woman he had in mind was someone he had seen several times in Riverside Park riding her bicycle at roughly the same time when he was doing his run. She wore a helmet, a mask, and dark glasses as she rode, but three or four times he had seen her leaning on her bike on the sidewalk, resting without her helmet, dark glasses, and mask. From a distance she seemed to have medium long brown hair, a pretty face, and an athletic build with long arms and legs. He guessed her height at around 5'7" or 5'8", about six inches shorter than him. He had not been close enough to see the color of her eyes. He was usually attracted or turned off by a woman's hands, eyes, and breasts, with breasts being less important for him than the other two physical features.

A few days before, Danny saw her resting on her bicycle without her helmet or mask. He sauntered over to catch a better view, but she suddenly swept her hair back into her helmet, replaced her mask, and rode away. For the last couple of weeks, Danny stood near the spot where she rode north every day in good weather at approximately 12:10 p.m. He would then do his run, but be sure to be back at the same place in front of a colorful flower garden at 1:10 p.m. where she would pass by on her return. Most of the time she rode speedily by, but sometimes she stopped, removed her helmet and mask, fixed her hair, and rested for a half minute or so before resuming her ride. The situation was extremely frustrating to Danny, because in this period of virus lockdown and social distancing, how could he ever meet her? Danny was determined to meet her. But how? The solution came to him one night around 3 a.m. when he got up to drink a glass of water and go to the bathroom.

Chapter 2

A few streets away a woman in her late twenties was preparing to go to Riverside Park to ride her bicycle on the pedestrian level and then head to the river bike path where she would peddle up to 125th Street or beyond. It was her daily athletic 'fix' which happily took her away from her work and got her outdoors every day when the weather was decent.

Jeanine "Ginny" Reynolds, 27 years old, had graduated from Columbia Law School this past June after spending her undergraduate years at Swarthmore and then teaching history for two years at The Masters School in Dobbs Ferry. Three years ago she entered law school with trepidation, but after a grueling start, she hit her stride and by the end of her first year, she was asked to join the Law Review. In the two summers before graduation, she had interned in a prestigious Manhattan law firm, successfully it seemed, because the firm had made her a generous offer to work full-time after she graduated. She had postponed the start of her new job until the early autumn, because she had arranged to travel to Europe in July and August with three law school friends, two women and a guy. This was their reward for graduating from law school. All four had good jobs awaiting them after graduation, Alissa and Nancy in corporate law firms in Manhattan and Theo at a human rights firm in Boston, his hometown.

Ginny and her friends had planned the trip meticulously, assigning two countries to each of the four travelers to reserve hotels, find great restaurants, select the major sites to see in the capitals, and discover an historically or aesthetically remote place that travel agents would be unlikely to recommend. In the drawing of straws, Ginny had received Spain and Switzerland as the countries where she would take the lead. Each of the travelers managed to find a native person in each country to guide them for a designated fee. The only exception was Switzerland, because Ginny's older brother Richard lived and worked in Geneva, and he agreed to guide them around Geneva and then to a charming small mountainous town, Leukerbad

(Loeche les Bains in French), in the Swiss German part of the Alps.

After spending a week in England (London, Cambridge, Oxford, and Coventry), they took the Chunnel to Paris where they spent a marvelous and gluttonous five days and then traveled by high speed trains in sequence to Italy, Spain, Germany, Austria, Slovakia, the Czech Republic, Hungary, and Switzerland. The four travelers visited fascinating sites, both in the capitals and in the selected remote areas, feasting their eyes on ancient towns, aristocratic castles, imposing mountains, and beautiful lakes. Ginny and the others came back culturally rejuvenated, but physically exhausted, each taking about two weeks to rest and reintegrate into American society before beginning their jobs in their respective law firms.

Ginny's firm specialized in corporate law, with each member of the firm expected to devote 6-8 hours a week to pro bono work for non-profit cultural organizations such as small theaters, ballet troupes, and music groups needing assistance to remain financially afloat. Ginny was assigned two struggling theatre companies, one in New York and the other in Philadelphia, as well as an up and coming ballet company in Austin,Texas. She was expected to visit these groups at least twice a year. Her main focus would be on large corporations, researching and making recommendations about legal and tax issues as member of a small team of experienced lawyers in the firm. Ginny as a newcomer was low on the office totem poll, but having spent two summers as an intern, she was familiar with the nature of the work and knew many members of the firm. As a beginning lawyer, she worked incredibly long hours, since that was what law firms expected of their new staff members. Working now from home in the virus lockdown, Ginny still labored arduously, with Zoom and FaceTime conferences taking place almost every day with her team members. She enjoyed working at home, dressing like a slob (except for the Zoom meetings), sleeping late (8 a.m.), working when she wished, and taking breaks for her daily bike ride in Riverside Park. When the weather got warmer, she contemplated going to Central Park to do the six mile jaunt around the park, some of it on steep hills.

Ginny had grown up in the Westchester suburb of New Rochelle.

She had an older brother and a younger sister, neither of whom lived in New York. Her brother Richard, four years older, worked for the United Nations in Geneva for the International Labor Organization (ILO), traveling throughout sub-Saharan African French-speaking countries, because he spoke French reasonably well after spending his college junior year in Paris. He traveled on missions to the former French colonies in West Africa, to Cameroon, Ivory Coast, Mali, Senegal, and the Central African Republic. Recently he had developed or inherited projects in former English colonies such as Kenya, Malawi, and Tanzania in East Africa, and he was contemplating how he could develop a project or two in conjunction with the Asia Division which would enable him to travel to India, China, Thailand, Laos, and Vietnam, places he had fantasized about, but hadn't yet visited.

Richard focussed on projects involving workers issues such as salary questions, union/labor interactions, and safety mechanisms in small-scale factories in developing countries. He had gotten an M.A. in development economics at Georgetown and had contemplated pursuing a doctorate to become a university professor. However, a fascinating job offer unexpectedly came from the father of his close friend at Georgetown, Amadou Bocoum of Senegal, whose father headed a department at the International Labor Organization in Geneva. He had met Richard during a visit to Georgetown and was impressed with his French-speaking ability and his intelligence in discussing the socio-economic problems facing the former French colonies in West Africa. Pere Bocoum offered Richard a one-year contract that would be renewed if there was satisfaction on both sides. Since Richard knew that most people would 'die' to receive such an offer at the age of twenty-eight, he decided to accept the ILO position and see if he could last a couple of years before falling back on his notion of pursuing a doctorate. The worst thing that could happen, he figured, was that he would obtain some practical development economics experience at the ILO, as well as a suitable topic or two to use for an eventual Ph.D. dissertation.

However, Richard not only enjoyed the work, but found the atmosphere at ILO headquarters greatly to his liking, particularly the interaction with an astonishing variety of people from different countries all over the world, a number of whom became close friends. He was also delighted with his 'find' of a brainy, attractive, good-humored Australian woman who worked in the World Health Organization (WHO) in Geneva. He had been happy to escort Ginny and her friends to Leukerbad, the beautiful Swiss German town in the Alps, as well as in and around Geneva, arranging a boat trip to the nearby small town of Nyon on Lake Geneva and a car ride to Ferney Voltaire just over the border in France where a lot of UN people lived, commuting daily to their offices in adjacent Geneva. Ginny was pleased that her brother, with whom she had never been particularly close over the years, was not only courteous and charming to her friends, but very affectionate with her. She also liked his Australian girl friend Carmen and offered to take her around New York City if she came to New York and New Rochelle next Christmas.

Ginny's younger sister, Susan, was a junior at UCal, Berkeley. The family's pet name for Susan was "the mistake on the lake," because she arrived eleven years after Richard and eight after Ginny, conceived presumably in the cabin on Lake Riptide in northern Vermont where the family spent a month each summer for the last thirty years. Susan didn't find that designation very amusing. In fact, she felt alienated from her parents who were clearly unprepared in their retirement years to look after a screaming child and then a sullen teen ager. Beginning in Susan's freshman year of high school, they began spending the winters in Playa del Carmen, Mexico, hiring an older unmarried woman cousin to stay in the house to be with Susan. Susan barely talked to the cousin who became reclusive, watching TV continually in her room. Understanding Susan's complaints, Ginny came frequently on weekends to be with her younger sister. When it came time for college, Susan decided to leave the east coast and go to California.

Early in her freshman year, she was lonely and depressed. She started therapy with a male therapist who told Susan that because she had very good relationships with her two older siblings, this could compensate for her feelings of isolation and low status with her parents. This notion made good sense to her, and she increased the frequency of her phone calls and messages to Ginny and Richard who responded in kind.

Aside from the issue of her parents, Susan talked frequently about men. After losing her virginity in her freshman year and having had a couple of brief flirtations in the early part of her sophomore year, she was now seeing a first-year graduate student pursuing a doctorate in European Political and Intellectual History at Stanford. Joshua (Josh) was assertive, even arrogant in his conversations and behavior with Susan. She related her anxieties to the therapist who advised her to speak up forcefully and challenge Josh if she felt that he was being macho or verbally aggressive towards her.

"If he cannot accept that you are a highly intelligent young woman who is not going to subordinate herself to him, then he is not worth keeping," the therapist said. "He sounds a little arrogant which could be a mask for insecurity. He probably needs some therapy himself, and you could make it a condition for your continuing to see him. However, for now, you should feel free to say anything you like to him and carefully monitor his reactions. Let's see if he can accept you as an equal."

Susan began to to challenge Josh on statements he made about politics, people, ideas, and cultural issues. Initially argumentative, he began to listen more carefully to her, and Susan told her therapist that Josh was respecting her intelligence and opinions much more than in the past. She reported that they had immense fun kidding around with each other, discussing serious political issues, going to concerts and films, doing physical workouts at the gym, and seeing friends together. Their love life also improved significantly. Joining the Stanford-UCal Democratic Club, they attended meetings and fund raising events in the fervent hope that the November election would consign President Trump to the dustbin of history. They both supported Californian Kamala Harris for Joe Biden's running mate.

In a long phone conversation with Ginny, Susan told her sister that she was in love with Josh and that they were talking about moving in together after the end of the pandemic. "I had hoped to bring him to New Rochelle in the summer to meet everybody, but that seems unlikely now. We're hunkered down together here in Berkeley, and who knows when the lockdown situation will end. So I suppose that we're already living together by choice."

"That's great," Ginny said. "I'm really happy for you, Suzie. Can I speak to Josh the next time you and I talk on the phone? I would like to tell him how lucky he is to be with you."

Susan laughed. "Let's wait a bit. I most definitely would like you to face time with him so that he can see what a beautiful older sister I have, but in your initial conversation with him, please talk about the virus or the weather, and do not extoll my supposed great virtues. He'll think that I set you up to do that."

"Fine, fine. I'll behave myself, and I won't allude to your great qualities. I'm not a complete dolt, you know."

"I know, I know. Tell me, though. How is your love life these days? Any old or new man, or are you too busy in your job and trapped in your apartment?"

"'Yes' as an answer to both questions. My job can be endless, but I have to focus on it even in lockdown time so that the partners see that I'm producing for the firm. No time to meet any new man, since I'm working like a dog, and also how would I meet someone in my solitary cave?"

"What about the guy you were seeing in the spring?

"My summer trip to Europe gave him freedom back in New York, and while he sent me some nice messages, he informed me two weeks before my return that he had begun to see another woman. To be honest, I felt relieved. And since then, I have met a few nice looking lawyers, but there was nobody who appealed to me very much. And now it's hopeless during the lockdown. Impossible to meet anybody new while in solitary confinement."

"The situation will change sometime soon, as we all hope. So be positive, Ginny, and have faith on all fronts."

"I love the fact that my younger sister, as smart and adorable as she is, is advising me on matters of the heart and of the soul in our virus-ridden time."

"Well...I told you that I've been seeing a therapist for almost two years, and it's made me calmer and more self-confident."

"That's terrific, and who knows, you may eventually talk me into seeing a therapist when this lockdown ends. I've always been so practical and self-motivated in my studies and now my career, and maybe I'm divorced somewhat from my feelings. I'd probably benefit by talking to a therapist again. I haven't done so since college."

After chatting for a few minutes longer, they promised to talk again over the weekend.

Hanging up the phone, Ginny thought about her love life over the last few years. What she hadn't told her sister was her flirtation with lesbianism that began six months ago.

Her relationship with an artist ended when he informed Ginny that while he liked her a lot, he found her emotionally cold and impossibly busy, and he had decided not to continue the relationship. Ginny was upset because she had thought that everything had been going well, even though she knew that her main focus in life was getting through law school and that she hadn't put much time or emotion into the relationship. She liked solidity, certainty, practicality, and men, she felt, were so mercurial, unpredictable and needy. Her last two relationships had fizzled without any warning, and who was to blame, she or the guys?

One day in the early spring last year, while walking in the West Village, Ginny passed some women sipping drinks and chatting on the sidewalk in front of a bar called the Pussycat Saloon. One of them smiled at Ginny and gestured to her to go into the bar. Ginny shrugged and walked inside. She sat on a stool at the bar and ordered a glass of sauvignon blanc.

After a few minutes, a woman with short dark hair sitting next to her reading a book asked Ginny if she had enough space.

"Yes, I'm fine," said Ginny.

The woman took off her glasses and put her book down on the counter. "Hi, I'm Sylvia," she said, putting her hand out for Ginny to shake. Ginny noticed that the title of the book was 'Romantic Poetry in the Post-Enlightenment Era'. "And your name is?"

"Jeanine. Well, actually Ginny which most people aside from my parents call me."

"Do you live in the Village, as I do, Ginny? I'm an assistant professor at N.Y.U.--18th to 20th century literature and poetry. So it's easy for me to walk from home to my office. How about you?"

"I live on the upper West Side, 75th Street off Riverside Drive. I'm in my final year of law school at Columbia."

"That's such a great area. Riverside Park is so pretty in the spring and summer. I like it better than Central Park. What brings you to the Village and to this place?"

I'll be honest with you. I recently broke up with my boyfriend who lives in the neighborhood down here, and since I had nothing to do this afternoon, I thought that I would take a walk in our old stomping ground."

"Interesting," said Sylvia. "You are aware, I would imagine, what type of place this is?"

Ginny smiled. "I can see. Could I ask you a few questions about this bar and the type of women who come here?"

"That sounds ominous," Sylvia said, smiling. "But, go ahead, and feel free not to keep it 'clean'. Just kidding." She put her hand on Ginny's arm, keeping it there for a few seconds.

"Can you tell me a little about yourself? Have you always…sorry, I don't know how to phrase it…."

"Always liked women? Is that what you're asking?"

"Yes, that's it."

Sylvia smiled and suggested that they move to a private booth. Sitting across from each other, she told Ginny that she had been 'so-called normal', even losing her virginity in her last year of high school to a 'hot older guy'. However in college at Michigan, she had had a couple of unfulfilling, even painful, relationships with men and was consoled emotionally and then physically by her college roommate. This was nineteen years ago, and since then she had been a "lesbo', as she put it. "I was in a long-term relationship with a great woman for a couple of years, but Jill split around six months ago to accept a job in Australia…And since then I have been looking, but not finding or 'acting'."

"That's interesting. I guess that I might be in the 'looking' stage."

"Let me make a suggestion. I have to go to my office now to meet with some students. Why don't you come to my apartment for dinner tomorrow evening, and we can continue schmoozing. Everything will be kosher, don't worry. I won't get you drunk or drug you. So no worries… You seem pretty smart and I'm not stupid. So we'll chat away and see how things go. I'll offer you my special lasagna, great wine, and good conversation. How about it?"

Ginny thought for a few seconds and then agreed. They exchanged phone numbers and addresses.

The next day Ginny was nervous all day, barely able to concentrate in her classes and in a meeting at the Law Review where she held an editorial position. She thought of canceling her 'date' with Sylvia, but around 6:00 p.m. she took the subway down to the Village and walked to Sylvia's apartment on Horatio Street. Sylvia gave Ginny a brief hug when she entered. Sylvia was wearing a multi-colored Mexican dress, large circular silver earrings, and gold rings on two fingers of each hand. They sat in the living room sipping wine and munching cheese and crackers. Then Sylvia ushered her to the circular kitchen table and served her lasagna, broccoli, salad, and more wine. Ginny found herself enjoying not only the food and the wine, but also the conversation on many subjects: the fiercely competitive nature of getting ahead in academia and in the legal profession, and stories about their respective families and upbringings. After dinner they moved back to the living room.

"So what do you think?" asked Sylvia. "Does the idea of being with a woman physically appeal to you?" She moved closer to Ginny on the couch, putting her hand on Ginny's shoulder.

"You're so easy to talk to," Ginny replied. "I wonder how it would be if we did anything physical. You would have to coach me and be pretty patient."

"I accept the challenge," Sylvia said, taking Ginny's face in her hands and touching her lips. Ginny froze. Sylvia hugged her gently, and Ginny slowly relaxed. Sylvia softly brushed her lips on Ginny's neck and then on her lips. Her tongue entered Ginny's mouth, and Ginny, hesitating, began to respond with her own tongue. They hugged and kissed softly and slowly for a few minutes, and then Sylvia rose to offer her hands to Ginny to stand up. They hugged and kissed, and Ginny let herself be guided by Sylvia to the bedroom…

Sylvia kept her hands on Ginny's back and slowly moved her right hand onto Ginny's left breast. Sylvia slowly undid the buttons of Ginny's shirt and then unstrapped her bra. She looked at Ginny's ample breasts, touching them with her hands and kissing the nipples.

"Very beautiful," she said.

Undoing her own shirt and bra, Sylvia placed Ginny's hands on her smaller breasts, and the two kept kissing with their lips and tongues. Sylvia undid the button of her pants which fell to the floor. Ginny tried to undo her buttons, but her fingers wavered, and Sylvia said: "Let me do it."

Soon they removed their shoes, undid their stockings, and were naked. They saw the whiteness of each other's flesh, the brown color of their nipples surrounded by a sea of white, as well as the glorious geometry of their lower bodies. Sylvia put some cream on her fingers and began to touch Ginny's vagina. Ginny moaned softly. Sylvia offered her the bottle, and Ginny adeptly put some cream on her fingers and began to rub Sylvia between her legs.

"Mmmm," murmured Sylvia, who hugged Ginny and pushed her down gently on the bed. When Ginny was on her back, Sylvia moved her legs apart, and began to lick Ginny's outer vagina. She slowly increased the pressure on her clitoris, Ginny beginning to moan softly. Sylvia began moving her finger deftly inside Ginny's vagina. Ginny lifted her lower body to accept Sylvia's mouth and fingers. Whimpering and moaning, Ginny thrust her lower body forward and after a few minutes, made a sharp noise of climatic release.

As Ginny lay there, Sylvia moved up next to her, hugging and kissing her gently on her cheeks and lips.

Ginny's face was red. She opened her eyes and gave a quizzical smile. "Shall I do that to you?"

Sylvia shook her head and smiled. "Not tonight. This evening is for you. Your baptism...Are you okay?"

"More than okay. I don't know how to describe it. Naturally I've had practice in pleasing myself, and men have done things, but I've never been pleasured by another woman. Was I clumsy? Did my inexperience show?"

"No, no. You did just fine. You were remarkably present, even though this was your first experience with a woman. And, I must say, you have a beautiful, responsive pussy." Sylvia gave it a last kiss, and Ginny shuddered.

"You're sure that I can't do something to you?"

Smiling, Sylvia said: "Another time. Hopefully soon."

"I'll have to think about all this…"

"I hope that you won't suddenly disappear," Sylvia said sharply. "That wouldn't be fair. Let's take it slowly, be friends mainly, and we can see how it goes as lovers. If any problems arise, we'll revert back to friendship. Okay?"

"I think so…Yes, it's okay. It was an amazing experience. I want to see you, for sure. Can we talk on the phone and maybe plan to have dinner in a few days?"

"Definitely. I hope that you will call me, but I'm not shy, and if I don't hear from you by Tuesday, I'll call you to arrange something. Let's have dinner on the upper West Side in your neighborhood. You choose the restaurant. Okay?"

"Fine. I think that I'd better go now." Ginny began to dress.

"Want me to walk you to the subway? I would be happy to do that."

"No. I think that I will take a taxi to commemorate my first experience with a woman. Not just any 'woman'. You!"

Thus began a six month period when Ginny and Sylvia saw each other every other week, meeting in Greenwich Village at Ginny's request, since she had a roommate and felt the Village to be more exotic, as well as safer than the upper West Side. They talked easily about a myriad of subjects and felt comfortable in restaurants and in Sylvia's bed where they hugged, kissed, touched, and licked each other, with Sylvia guiding Ginny to do things on her body that provoked immense sexual satisfaction. Following her lead, Ginny began to learn what turned Sylvia on, and Sylvia knew exactly what to do with Ginny to induce shivering feelings and big orgasms.

"I thought that I would have more trouble with this than I am," Ginny said on their fourth 'date'."

"Maybe you're a natural born lesbian," Sylvia said a little mockingly.

"I'm not sure about that…but it does feel good to be with someone as sexually experienced as you."

"Everyone is different," said Sylvia. "I try to do what you like, what pleases you, and I lead you to do what pleases me."

"It's all very logical, as you explain it. I think that I'm lucky to have found such an easy person like you. I would bet that there are many difficult, insecure women out there. You seem very secure."

"I hope so. It took me a long time to accept that I really didn't like to be with men, that women were more to my liking. I've told you that I had a two year affair with Jill which ended only because she went to Australia. If she had stayed, I suspect that we'd still be together."

Ginny hugged Sylvia and kissed her on the mouth softly. "Lucky me that she left and that you approached me in the bar."

"Yes. I feel lucky too. You are my first involvement since Jill left for Melbourne. Ironically Jill came to DC with me to meet my family about a month before she accepted the job offer and took off."

"You've mentioned that it was difficult for you to tell your family about your predilections…"

"Yes, it was difficult. I waited for years to tell them while they kept asking me why I wasn't finding a nice man to marry. I kept making excuses about men, inventing phony relationships while I gave complicated reasons why they didn't work out. Finally my sister asked me point blank if I preferred women to men. I told her the truth and she was great about it, becoming my ally and helping me to tell my parents and my other two siblings. It was tough initially, but I brought Jill home one weekend, and Jill behaved beautifully, asking all the right questions and charming the pants off of them. She had a separate bedroom and made sure not to be at all physical with me in front of my parents. After that they seemed to have accepted me for who I am."

"How nice. Jill must be a very clever person."

"She is….But so are you. And I would like you to come to DC with me in late March for the party to celebrate my sister's engagement."

"Are you sure?"

"Yes. You're smart like Jill. I know that you'll be okay with my family. Of course you'll have to keep your lovely hands off me."

Ginny smiled. "Okay. It'll be tough, but I agree. Let's plan it. Can we go to some of the museums which I haven't seen yet? I'm thinking of the FDR Presidential Library and the National Museum of African-American History and Culture."

"Sure. It's a deal, but I'd like you to come with me to the US History Museum which has all those original documents of the American revolution, as well as the Air and Space part of the Smithsonian. I love looking at the Kitty Hawk suspended high up and reading about the history of early flight and the Wright brothers."

"Of course. It sounds as if we will have several history lessons jammed together, as well as great fun. I hope that your family will like me."

"They will adore you as I do. Let's book our train tickets and get the ball rolling."

However, the trip never took place, because the coronavirus era intervened, disrupting the U.S. and the entire world and preventing them from going to Sylvia's parents home in Washington, D.C. in mid-March.

....

Since Sylvia could teach her classes remotely, she decided to go to DC to help her parents manage their health problems, as well as organize food shopping and delivery and the cleaning of the house. She kept in touch with Ginny by phone, emails, texts, and the mutual sending of cartoons, humorous virus-related songs cum singing/acting performances, as well as anti-Trump caricatures and presidential declarations minimizing the extent and impact of the virus. The day before, Trump had had the audacity to divert attention from his irresponsible and shameful behavior of 'virus malign neglect' (Sylvia's term) and outrageously blaming former President Obama for some vague, nonsensical 'conspiracy'.

"The man is insane," Sylvia said to Ginny on the phone. "If people die because of his total focus on himself and his neglect of the spreading pandemic, he should be charged with murder. The death rate is increasing like crazy, you know."

"I know. I know. The Law School is mobilizing remotely to prepare a legal challenge to Trump for 'malicious neglect' of the early stage of the pandemic which has allowed it to spread throughout the country, with New York exploding with virus cases and related deaths, with it still being called the epicenter."

Sylvia and Ginny found that they had plenty to talk about long distance, aside from the virus. They joked a lot with each other. Sometimes they dressed up in wacky clothes and silly hats and talked baby talk to one another, provoking giggles and laughter. When one or both felt adventuresome, that is, sexually turned on, they had phone sex, face timing each other's faces, breasts, and vaginas, breathing heavily and touching themselves, sometimes to the point of orgasmic relief. A few times they watched lesbian porn films that excited them and led to simultaneous self-satisfaction.

One evening Sylvia said: "You probably forgot that you were going to come to the Gay Pride Parade in the Village with me."

"Right. I did forget, but it's canceled now, isn't it?

"Yah. It always attracts a huge crowd of participants cavorting with each other, as well as a bundle of gawking observers from out of town. Can't happen now, but next year I'd like you to walk with me in the parade."

"Of course I will, Sylvia. Do you dress up? Do you wear a provocative costume?"

"No. I've always played it straight, wearing conservative feminine clothes. However, you can dress any way you want, even as a wild lesbian, if that turns you on."

Ginny laughed. "We'll see. Maybe I'll create a women's lib costume that will be an amalgam of Simone de Beauvoir, Betty Friedan, and Gloria Steinem. That would be quite a challenge."

"Great idea, my love. I'll help you dress up in a melange of accoutrements. Oh, shit, my mother is whining for attention. Talk to you tomorrow."

Ginny was now alone in her apartment, because her roommate had fled town to her family's house in upstate Vermont. She worked long hours researching legal cases and holding meetings with her colleagues on Zoom. For relief from work, she read the New York Times in the early mornings, watched Governor Cuomo's daily briefings, Dr. Fauci's ominous, yet realistic pandemic-related pronouncements, Judy Woodruff's news hour at 7 p.m., dinner at 8 p.m., and Rachel Maddow afterwards. When she was fed up reading or hearing the horrible news about the virus or U.S. politics, she began to read Stendhal's 'The Red and the Black', buying Marquez's 'Love in the Time of Cholera' as a follow-up novel to read. She talked frequently on the phone with her parents, her siblings, her close friends, and Sylvia. She turned down two friends' invitations to walk in Central Park, but she promised herself that she would accept their invitations in a week or two. Though her solitary life was repetitive, it was reasonably fulfilling from early morning to bedtime with her work, novel reading, and daily bike riding outside in good weather and inside on her stationary bike in cold, rainy, or snowy weather.

At 11:50 a.m. on May 12, 2020, Ginny shut her computer off and began to dress for her bike ride in Riverside Park.

Chapter 3

A few streets away, Danny Miller put on his running shorts and shoes to run in the park. He was nervous, because today was the day when he would put into action his plan to meet the attractive woman he had seen riding her bicycle in Riverside Park. He understood what he needed to do to meet her, but there was no way to predict how she would react. The worst case scenario was that she would ignore him or even scorn him. The best case would be that she would commiserate and endeavor to help him. He flipped a quarter and said to himself: heads, I win; tails, I lose. The coin came out 'heads', and he breathed more easily. He was still very nervous. 'What the hell', he thought. 'If I fuck up, I fuck up. Life is short, and one must take chances, even ridiculous ones, if one feels strongly. If I screw up this time, so what. Life will go on'. His nervousness increased, however, as he walked out of his building and began a slow jog en route to the park.

Ginny had left on her bike ride some minutes before. She felt strong today, and after a slow start on the pedestrian walkway down the hill at 79th Street, she rode quickly, heading left to the path bordering the Hudson River, giving a beautiful view of the cliffs and buildings across the river in New Jersey. Finally great weather, Ginny thought, after we've had such miserable weather in April and early May. We lockdown types deserve to have great weather right now. Maybe I can begin to work on a mild sun tan, she mused. This would require additional time sitting on a bench in the park, reading and/or meditating, and with her onerous work schedule, she didn't see how she could spare additional time outdoors. It's ridiculous, she thought. If the weather is like this tomorrow, I'm going to sit on a park bench in the sun with my work for at least an hour, if not longer. Having made this decision, she peddled quickly, enjoying the mild breeze lapping her cheeks. Riding next to the West Side Highway, she noticed an increase in the number of cars moving in both directions, as compared to the previous week. Maybe things were opening up, not just upstate in rural areas, but in densely populated downstate New York City as well. Wishful thinking…She vowed once again in her mind not to violate the social distancing precept when she went out walking or food shopping a few times a week. On her bike she was far apart from other riders. So no problem there....

Although the river path snaked up to the George Washington Bridge, when she arrived at 140th Street, she turned around and rode south. Arriving at West 97th Street, she pedaled by the dormant clay tennis courts and rode up a path leading to the pedestrian walkway. She passed a deserted playground, as well as beautiful flower beds attended by elderly volunteers. A woman watering a multi-colored flower garden waved to Ginny as she passed. Ginny waved back and continued riding.

As she approached a second playground, she slowed down to give space to a few mothers and fathers leading their small children towards the promised land of the playground. She smiled at the sight of the small children running on their little legs towards the swings. Then she began to speed up again, moving quickly towards the hill leading down to West 79th Street.

Suddenly a runner whom she hadn't seen ran into her bicycle and fell down, emitting a scream of pain.

"Oh, my God," Ginny shouted, seeing blood on the kneecap of the runner's left leg. She got off her bicycle. "I'm so sorry. Are you okay?"

"I think I'm alive," Danny Miller said, holding onto his bloody leg. "I'm lucky that you weren't going full speed. Oh, my....This is painful," he said, clutching the bottom part of his leg.

"Can you walk"? Ginny asked. "Please...let me help you get up." She bent over to offer her hand to Danny. He took it and buckled over, falling down again.

"I'm sorry," he said. "I'm being clumsy, but it does hurt quite a lot."

"You fell down hard," Ginny said. "I'm worried that you might have badly injured your knee. Can you walk?"

"Barely," he said, hobbling. "Would you mind if I hold on to your bike?"

"No, of course not. What shall we do? Are you in great pain? We should get you to a doctor. Maybe to a hospital emergency room."

"If I go there, it will be hours, and I have an important work call with my partners at 3 p.m." Then he said: "There's a CityMD branch on Broadway at 88th Street where you just walk in with no appointment, and excellent doctors see you. I've been there before, and they do X-rays. The only problem is that I don't know if I can make it there on my own."

"Listen. I feel so badly. I wasn't looking, and it's definitely my fault. Would you like me to come with you?

"That would be great. So nice of you. If I can hold on to your handlebars and if we can move slowly, I think that I can make it."

"Let's head there now. I also have a group meeting but not until 5 p.m."

Danny held on to the handlebars of Ginny's bike, walking awkwardly alongside her. He noticed her crystal clear blue eyes and her long slender hands which gave him a shudder inside. "I guess that we should know each other's names," he said. "I'm Danny Miller. And you?"

"Ginny Reynolds. Do you live close to the park like me?" She felt better now that the runner was chatting, and it appeared that he hadn't broken or fractured his leg or knee.

"Yes, on West 77th Street a half block from the park. And you?"

"Two streets down, on West 75th between West End and Riverside."

"Amazing. We live just two blocks apart. Strange that we haven't seen each other before, but that's New York where one often doesn't even know one's neighbors on the same floor. Plus the new social distancing keeps everybody away from each other these days. How are you managing through this lockdown? Maybe we should put our masks back on?"

"Yes, yes. Let's definitely do that." Seeing his face, blond hair, and blue eyes, she thought to herself: 'Mmm. Handsome guy; probably involved with a nice looking girlfriend. Ginny, stop thinking stupid stuff'. They walked slowly holding onto the bicycle handle bars on either side, Danny hobbling, accentuating the mild pain that he felt in his right knee.

He was extremely happy, because his ploy had worked, and this young woman whom he had found super attractive from a distance also seemed to be a decent, caring person. She could easily have ridden off, but she had stopped, and she was now accompanying him to the doctor. So far things couldn't be better, he said to himself.

Moving slowly up Riverside Drive, Danny asked her how she was doing during the lockdown.

"I graduated Columbia law school last June, and I'm a beginning law 'slave', to define it accurately." She named her firm which was one of the prominent second tier law firms in the city, but he said that he hadn't heard of it. He told her briefly about his company, his role as founder and president, and how he was coping working at home.

"It's bizarre," Ginny continued. "And who knows how long this solitary situation will go on. I think that you and I are among the lucky ones, because we at least have jobs and work that we like and can do it at home. My law school friends are in that situation, but I know a few people who have been laid off or furloughed without pay. They're having a tough time."

"Understandable. It's so depressing to read about all the layoffs, the restaurant, theatre, ballet, and film closings. So many desperate people who cannot pay rent or feed their families. I feel particularly sorry for the poor actors, opera singers, and ballet performers, not to mention the abundance of support staffs who have lost their jobs. And we have such a bizarre, malevolent president who initially denied that there was a pandemic and then has refused to accept blame or responsibility for the deaths and the increasing economic misery. One day Trump praises experts like Fauci and the next day ignores or blames him for telling the hard truth. Sorry. I shouldn't talk politics because I don't know your stance on things. You may even like Trump. I know a couple of people who do."

"Are you kidding? I can't stand that narcissistic bully and all those sycophantic Republican Senators fearful of alienating him because he can seriously jeopardize their re-election with a couple of negative tweets. These past four years have been a terrible time. All those blatant lies. Trump undermining our NATO allies, sucking up to Kim Jong Un of North Korea with no positive result, talking nicely about the Chinese president one day and blaming China for creating the virus the next. Denying climate change; undermining our role in the U.N.; wanting to take us out of the World Health Organization; appointing right-wing judges to the Supreme Court and conservative, unqualified judges proposed by that evil Republican Senate leader Mitch McConnell. Dancing with Putin who undoubtedly holds damning evidence of Trump's financial corruption and womanizing in the U.S., as well as in Russia and a person who helped to steal the election from Hilary in 2016. I could go on and on, but it's already giving me a headache."

"I couldn't agree more," Danny said. "We're on the same wave length completely." He hesitated for an instant and then said: "You mentioned that you went to Columbia Law School. I went to Columbia Business School. Do you know that Trump just called Columbia University, our alma mater, "a liberal hellhole'?"

"Did he really? That's a compliment."

"Definitely so. If we don't get a Democrat into office in November, this country will sink even further into the muck. Do you think Biden can win?"

"He has to," she said. "Remember how much Hilary was ahead in the polls and then lost through her own mistakes. Biden has to get a strong vice presidential candidate and hit back at Trump's personal attacks and insults. So far Biden seems timid, uncertain. However, he must win in November, or our democracy will be jeopardized if Trump and his Republican allies get another four years to appoint conservative judges who could be around for decades." She hesitated for a second. "Ruth Bader Ginsburg. Can she last another four years? I doubt it. So there has to be a Democratic president in office to appoint her successor. In my darker moments when I think that Trump may win, I fantasize leaving the country. Of course I would have to give up my job which I don't want to do. Maybe I could convince them to let me start up a branch office in Paris."

"That would be pretty nice, I would imagine."

"For sure. I spent my junior year in Paris and speak French fairly well even now. I'd be game for that." Danny ruminated for a few seconds on the thought of Ginny leaving the country and didn't like that idea at all. They talked a few more minutes about the lamentable political scene in the country and arrived at the CityMD ground floor office.

"Thanks so much, Ginny," Danny said, feigning intense pain in his leg. "I couldn't have done this without you. I guess that you have to leave now."

"I think that you'll be taken quite soon because I see only one other person waiting here. I'll stay around and help you get back to your apartment, if this doesn't take too long and if they don't insist that you go to the hospital."

"That's not going to happen, I'm sure. The pain is easing up, though it's still there," he said, wincing. In his mind he was desperate to make sure that they exchanged their contact information or he might never see her again.

An attendant in a white coat appeared. "Daniel Miller," he said.

Danny looked at Ginny. "I doubt if this will take very long. You're sure that you can stay and help me get home?"

"Yes, yes. I can wait for awhile."

"If for any reason you have to leave, could you please leave your contact information with the front desk? You've been so kind, and I want to send you some flowers."

"No, no need for that. I caused the accident, and the least that I can do is to stick around to help you get back to your apartment."

Danny nodded and left with the medical assistant.

Thirty-five minutes later he reappeared. Ginny was checking her cell phone with a magazine draped over her lap.

"So?" she asked.

"Nothing broken. A nice bandage on my knee, as you see, and some pain medication. I'm really lucky. It could have been so much worse, according to the doctor."

"Great." She got up and opened the door for him.

Danny held on to the bicycle hobbling down Broadway. They agreed to move to Riverside Drive where there would be fewer people.

"So," he said, as they reached the sidewalk along the park at 88th Street. "What kind of cases are you working on now?"

She described a couple of cases and mentioned her pro bono work with the three non-profits.

"I wish that my firm was a non-profit so that we could get your firm's help in some knotty legal problems that we are currently having."

"Tell me about it," Ginny said.

Danny described a couple of legal issues that his company was currently involved in. She offered some thoughts which he said were useful.

"Your company, Allegria, sounds pretty cool as a contemporary tech firm. The stuff that you are doing seems relevant to older folks. My dad, for example, could use some upgrading of his tech skills and his ability to access Netflix, Hulu, and the like. Do you take on individual clients or just companies?"

"We haven't done any contract work just with individuals so far," Danny replied. "But It's amazing that you should ask, since one of my current projects is exploring how to tailor our product to individual subscribers. I would be happy to share some of my thoughts with you to see if it applies to your dad."

"Sure," she said, as they were approaching West 77th Street, Danny's block. Crossing the drive, they continued to a building halfway up the block.

"Looks like I'm home. What an adventure so far...."

"Tell me truthfully," Ginny said. "Are you sure that you're okay? You're still hobbling and you must be experiencing some pain."

"Yes, there is some pain, and I won't be able to jog now, but the doctor assured me that I should be able to run again in 2-3 weeks. So until then I will do my weights and calisthenics in my apartment without any aerobics. I hope that I don't get too fat in the next couple of weeks."

"You don't seem like the fat type," she said.

"I was chubby as a kid, but fortunately I loved playing sports starting at an early age. These days, running, basketball, and tennis have kept me in reasonably decent shape."

"You're a tennis player then?"

"Yes, I am. I was on the high school team and then on the freshman team at Tufts. Before the onset of the virus, I was playing twice a week at the Manhattan Plaza Tennis Club way over on West 43rd Street with a regular partner, but he skipped town to stay with his family in Montauk. And the club is closed now anyway. Do you play?"

"I played in high school and then on the team at Swarthmore. I wasn't in the top four, but I did play doubles and occasionally some singles."

"Wow, that's great. Maybe we could play when my leg improves and the weather becomes warm. When my club closed, I got a permit to play on city courts in Central Park and Riverside Park, but they're also closed now. I've been hoping the city courts will reopen, but no sign of that yet. It could be a long dreary summer without tennis."

"That would be unpleasant. I also have a partner, but no way that we can play now."

"I have a car which I park in a garage just north of Columbia University," Danny said, "and I occasionally drive to Fort Lee or Englewood to play tennis. The courts are located outside high schools, and I'm sure that they're open even now. I'll naturally have to wait until my knee improves."

Looking at her phone, Ginny said: "Wow, it is already 3 p.m. I'd better get home to prepare for my Zoom meeting."

"Could you please give me your contact information, and I'll be happy to do the same. In fact, here's my card. You will see the weird logo on the other side of King Harald Bluetooth of medieval Denmark. He is famous in Danish and Christian history in that he adopted Christianity in the 9th century in order to unite his kingdom. Our company is trying to simplify and adapt bluetooth technology to different situations, and we thought that this logo would symbolize what we are trying to do and even be attractive."

Ginny took the card. "Looks intriguing," she said, writing her contact information on the back of one of his cards.

"Good-bye, Ginny." He bumped elbows with her in lieu of shaking hands. "Thanks again for your kindness and support." She rode off.

In his apartment Danny jumped up and down and immediately hurt his lower leg. "Asshole," he said to himself, hobbling to the fridge to take out a Heineken beer. Sitting on the sofa, he ruminated over what had just happened. He had deliberately run into Ginny's bike, had even hurt himself in the process. But it was worth it. Now that he had met her, he could contact her easily. He didn't want to appear overly aggressive or needy, though, and it would be better if she initiated contact. But she might be traditional, and therefore it was up to him as the man to contact her.

The following day he went to a nearby flower shop and bought a large collection of exquisite flowers which the sales person wrapped in plastic tied with elegant red and blue ribbons. He wrote on a small card: "To Ginny. Many thanks for your kindness yesterday. Danny." Walking to West 75th Street near Riverside Drive, he handed the flowers to the doorman in Ginny's building, instructing him to inform Jeanine Reynolds.

"Oh, Ginny, you mean. Sure...I'll let her know."

Danny returned to his apartment. He worked intensively until 3 p.m. and then headed to the park, walking slowly on his slightly damaged leg. He sat on a bench reading his novel 'The Plague' by Albert Camus.

Around 6, back at home, he received the following text: "Danny, thanks so much for the lovely flowers. Not necessary, of course, but much appreciated. Ginny."

Half an hour later, Danny texted back: "Thanks for your thanks. My leg a bit better today. I went to the park and read on a bench. Since I can't run right now, could I induce you to join me tomorrow at 6 to social distance on a bench in Riverside Park at 78th Street?"

A reply came ten minutes later: "Sure. See you then."

The previous evening Sylvia had called Ginny. As they chatted, Ginny told her that something unusual had happened during her bike ride in Riverside Park. She told the story of a runner crashing into her bicycle, followed by the trip to City MD.

"Quite an incident," Sylvia said. "What's the guy like?"

"Nice enough. Seems to be a go-getter, president of a small start-up. He gave me his card. Here it is. The company is called "Allegria." Deals with bluetooth technology, a term that I've heard in connection with Bitcoin, but I don't know anything about it."

"Is this guy good looking"

"Not bad. Decent looking…"

"Should I be jealous?"

"Sylvia. What nonsense. I'm just telling you about the unusual thing that happened today. I probably won't ever see him again."

"That I doubt, but let's see. Now for us. Any interest in some sexual repartee and then some face and pussy time action?"

"It's been awhile since we had some phone sex. Let's go for it."

And they did.

Chapter 4

The next day at 6 p.m. Danny was sitting on a bench in Riverside Park reading his novel. He had pulled down his mask so that his face was visible.

"Hello, Invalid. You don't seem to be suffering too much." Ginny was wearing her mask.

"A masked woman, maybe the Lone Ranger's female sidekick. Hello, Ginny. I left lots of space for you to sit on the other side of the bench."

"Good. Social distancing rules us all. How is your knee today?"

"Doing better. The pain has eased. I did some exercise indoors, and that made me feel better."

"It's amazing, isn't it, how exercise can make one feel so much better, not just physically, but psychically as well. I used to go to the gym at least four times a week, but not now."

"Which gym did you go to?" Danny asked.

"The West Side Y."

"That was my gym also. Good location and excellent equipment. I never saw you there. We must have had different schedules."

"Yes, my schedule varied," she said. "Sometimes I went at 6-6:30 a.m. before work, but mostly after work as late as 8 p.m."

"That's why I never saw you. Our office is reasonably close to the

Y, and I mostly went at noon or early afternoon if work permitted. Since I was the boss, I didn't set too many meetings after 11:30 a.m. so as to allow me to hit the gym at noon or 12:30. So what do you do now when it rains or snows and you can't bike outside?"

"I have a stationary bike in my apartment."

"Me too."

She smiled. "It looks as if we're both gym rats or exercise mavens."

"Fanatics, maybe, but nothing wrong with that, especially during this lockdown. It's important, even critical, to be physically active now. We're both lucky to be able to work from home. Imagine how many millions of poor souls have lost their jobs and are languishing at home without money coming in for rent or food."

"Definitely," she said, frowning. "It's such a tragedy. I contribute to some food banks, but I should probably be doing much more."

"I'm sure that you're doing what you can." She didn't reply and he then said: "I guess that with your legal work you're really busy during the day and probably also the evenings. I had, still have, a close friend who compared his first year of working in a law firm to life in a penal colony. "

Ginny laughed. "I can relate to that. I work at what is called a white-shoe firm, supposedly very chic, and to maintain the high standards, my superiors are continually judging a beginning attorney like me in terms of both quantity and quality. So I have to grind away, even in the covid period. You're the president of your company, and so you can set the scene. I imagine that you also must be judging your underlings on the basis of the quality and quantity of the work they accomplish."

"Definitely. I even have to lean gently on one of my partners who is in a bit of a depression in his lockdown state at home. I tell him that he'll get out of his funk if he can channel his depressive thoughts to his work, do regular exercise, and reach out to his family and friends more than he has done so far. I call him twice a day to see how he's doing emotionally and psychologically." Danny smiled at her. "However, since the work day is presumably over for both of us, though maybe not for you, let's talk about something other than work".

"Cool. You go first."

After hesitating for a second, he said: "I'll start with a question. Where did you grow up?"

That question elicited a reasonably long reply and she posed the same question to Danny. They talked about their youth and their high school days in New Rochelle and West Hartford. Then they branched out to the subject of their parents and their siblings.

"My married brother, Joel, is a great guy," Danny said, "but he's definitely a bit bourgeois."

"What do you mean by that?"

"He's always been career and money oriented, and luckily for him, he has succeeded pretty well, now working for a big insurance company and rising upward through the ranks."

"Sounds good, if that's his objective."

"Definitely. I just wish that he had more time to play, to go to the theatre, and to play tennis on the weekends, but he rarely accepts. He was a far better player as a kid and in high school than I was. I invite him to meet me after work in the city for dinner and to play tennis on the weekend, but he rarely accepts. He seems to be working all the time, leaving early in the morning and often getting back late for dinner. Hey, it's his life. He has a nice wife and adorable kids, and I'm very happy to be an uncle. I take that role pretty seriously by going to South Nyack at least once, if not twice, a month to get jumped on by Anya and Andrew and take them to the playground to play sports."

"That sounds like great fun."

"It is. It makes me want to have kids myself one day." He immediately felt that he shouldn't have mentioned this thought to Ginny, since she might be frightened off by such a notion.

But she replied: "I can relate to that. I've decided that if I don't have a kid by the time I am in my late thirties, I will adopt or I will get someone to impregnate me."

Danny laughed. He asked her how old she was. "Twenty-seven," she replied.

"That's a decade away," he said. "You have plenty of time to…" He didn't complete the sentence. "I'm 32 and I still feel pretty young. But tell me about your brother and sister."

"Sure. My brother Richard lives in Geneva and is working for the United Nations there. He's seeing a terrific Australian woman whom I met last summer. Hopefully she'll come to the States with him at Christmas time. And my younger sister Susan is an undergrad at Berkeley. She's locked down with a guy and maybe something will come of that."

"They each seem to have nice relationships. Your family's hopes are probably centered on you to get married and produce offspring."

Ginny laughed loudly. "They may have a long time to wait."

"Really? The full decade when you leap into adoption or impregnation?"

"Forgot what I said. Let's just stay in the present. We have little choice anyway, given the situation."

"I agree. Let's change the topic. What do you like to do when you're not working or working out? Do you go to the theatre, museums, films?"

They talked for another hour about their cultural interests, including theatre performances, serious plays and musicals, classical and jazz concerts, films (they agreed that "Casablanca" was their mutual top choice); and the abundance of amazing museums in Manhattan. The sun began to set, and it was getting dark.

"Getting difficult to see right now," Danny said. "It was really nice talking with you, Ginny. How about we continue tomorrow at 6 p.m.? At this spot again."

She thought for a minute and said: "Tomorrow will be an intense work day for me, with phone calls galore and a couple of Zoom meetings, and so I can't promise to be here at 6."

"No problem," Danny said. "I'll come here with my novel and if you show up, fine. If not, I can see you the following day."

"Okay. That's fine. Either tomorrow or the day after."

The following day Ginny didn't show up. Nor did she appear the day after. Nervously walking in circles in his apartment, Danny decided to call her at 8:30 pm.

"Ginny, it's me. Danny. You didn't show, and I thought that I would call you. I hope that's okay."

"Endless work these two days. Kept me from biking today and from meeting you."

"Is now a decent time for you to talk?"

"Yes, it's fine. I'm exhausted mentally from pouring over a couple of law cases, and I could definitely use some conversation on other subjects. A couple of my friends called earlier, and I told them to call me later this evening. So if a call or two comes in, I may have to interrupt our conversation to let them know that I'm busy and that I'll call them back."

"Perfectly fine. That might happen to me as well. I use my land line for business and my cell phone for friends. If one of my buddies or even my mother calls me, I'll put them off until later."

"I need to decompress. Maybe you could tell me what you did today. You probably went to the park at 6 p.m."

"Even earlier. I was done with my work by mid afternoon, and I took a rest and headed out at 4:30 p.m. with my book. It was great to people-watch and kid-watch. I'm still amazed how many people don't wear face masks. Not just young people like us who have been accused of arrogance and lack of caring for others, but even older people. I would say that a third of the people I saw today were bare-faced. Runners, bikers, parents with small kids. What's wrong with them? Don't they know the expression 'In Fauci We Trust'? Dr. Fauci advocates face masks and social distancing and claims that if the bozos reopen things too soon, there will be a second wave of the epidemic which could be even worse than the present one. He even says that we're still in the first wave."

"Yes, I know. While we would all like to reopen society and re-invigorate the economy, if that happens too quickly and the virus intensifies, we'll have a worse situation than we have now."

They discussed the absence of a surefire virus cure and the possible need to quarantine and social distance well into the fall and maybe into the following year.

"I'll really freak out if the current situation is extended," Ginny said. "You cannot be enjoying the solitude, the inability to see your family and friends. Its abnormal."

"It sucks. I'm just accepting it because there is no sense in banging my head against the wall and saying "woe is me" over and over. However, I do have my moments of complete boredom and mild despair."

They continued to talk on the phone, with Ginny getting interrupted twice and Danny once. After an hour Danny said that he shouldn't be monopolizing Ginny's evening so much and perhaps they should hang up and call people back. "I'll be in the park tomorrow, same time, same place. Will you come?"

"Yes. Even if there is a tsunami internally in my office, I'll be there. I also can't stand being cooped up."

"Good. I remember you calling me 'Invalid' the other day. I now have a new name for you."

"Really. What is it?"

"Florence, as in Nightingale. You were my medical savior, and so I can officially refer to you as 'Florence'."

Ginny laughed loudly. "Okay, 'Invalid'. My new nickname is 'Florence'. I'll try to come up with a better name than 'Invalid' for you. Bye bye."

One of Ginny's calls had come from Sylvia. She had decided not to tell Sylvia about her newfound communication with Danny, since Sylvia was capable of being very jealous. So the Golden Rule of Silence would prevail for now.

The next day Ginny appeared in the park just after 6 p.m. The conversation flowed easily on serious and on light topics, as before. Every day that week and the following one, the two sat together on the bench jabbering away. If it rained and they couldn't meet, Danny called Ginny on the phone in the evening. Once she called him.

"Have you ever gone out with a left-handed guy?" Danny asked her one day in the park.

"Can't remember if I have. What is so special about being left-handed?"

"Good question. I'm a lefty, for one thing. It's a select fraternity which includes Napoleon Bonaparte, Bill Clinton, Barak Obama, and of course, many tennis and basketball players of renown. Think Rafael Nadal who was born a righty, but his father and uncle forced him as a young kid to play tennis lefty because it would give him a big advantage later on. That certainly worked out fantastically well. Regarding lefties in basketball, think Bill Russell."

"Who's Bill Russell?"

"The guy who was selected by the fifty top players as the most outstanding player of all time, the one they would want on their teams above anyone else. A defensive and rebounding center, he played with the Boston Celtics in the 1950s-60s, and they won ten championships with him. A lefty, of course."

"Were you always left-handed?"

"My mother told me that when I was three or four years old, she tried to switch me to be a righty, but I kept putting the pencil right back into my left hand. She eventually gave up."

Ginny laughed. "You were undoubtedly a cute kid, and now I learn, a stubborn one who wanted to stay a lefty."

"It used to be a real stigma. Now, of course, it's completely accepted. However, not all lefties possess the remarkable quality that I have."

"Oh, yeah. What's that?"

"If someone is eating or writing or throwing with their left hand, I pick it up immediately. At a restaurant, watching a film or t.v., seeing someone throw a ball...Whenever I see a lefty, it instantly registers in my brain. For example, you see the guy on the bench down there? He just scratched his face with his left hand. Maybe it's a bit eerie, but I sense immediately which hand a person is using. I know that it's a completely useless talent, but it's something that I can't help noticing."

"That's interesting, as long as you don't flaunt your lefty knowledge all the time, since that would be boring. I'll give you a chance or two to demonstrate your innate recognition of left handedness, as long as you surprise me with it."

"Deal," he replied, and threw a tennis ball at her lefty. She caught it with her right hand and threw it back to Danny with her left.

Chapter 5

Both Ginny and Danny began to tell their siblings and their close friends about each other.

"Hey, Joel. What's up?" Danny's brother gave a quick recitation on the phone about his lockdown situation in South Nyack, touching on the boredom of his wife and their efforts to find inventive things to do with their two children. "Actually I'm enjoying having this time with the kids. It's a welcome change from my normal obsessive work schedule. So that part is great… Anything new with you, Danny"

"Yeah. Something interesting. I met a new woman that I like a lot. I literally ran into her in Riverside Park while I was running and she was riding her bike. She took me to CityMD to have my knee examined, and we've been talking ever since. She's a lawyer working at home now."

"A unique way to meet someone, you crazy guy," Joel said. "Amazing that you meet a classy woman during the lockdown. How many guys languishing at home would love to be in your shoes?"

"A lot probably, but I'm not sharing her. We meet in Riverside Park almost every day and shoot the breeze about an endless variety of topics. She grew up in New Rochelle, and her parents still live there."

"Across the Hudson River. I considered living there before choosing South Nyack. You know that New Rochelle had one of the worst early coronavirus situations. People in a synogogue got it from an infected rabbi, my friend Noel who lives there told me. Cuomo called in the National Guard to enforce people staying indoors, and it worked. After a couple of weeks, no new cases of the virus appeared in New Rochelle…Tell me, though… have you already…'done the nasty'?"

"Shit, Joel. That's an archaic expression. You mean: have I gotten into her pants?" Laughing loudly, he said: "We haven't even kissed yet. We just sit on a bench in the park observing the social distancing rule with our masks on and sometimes off. But I sense that the day is coming when my inner beast will emerge."

"Keep your inner beast tamed for now, Danny. Don't rush things. Always a good principle to take it slowly. Good luck on that and on everything else, Danny, and keep me posted. And think about coming here soon. Big hugs, my boy."

"And the same to you and to Barbara, Anya, and Andrew."

Ginny was in close contact with her siblings, speaking with Richard in Geneva once every two weeks and with Susan in Berkeley once or twice a week.

"Richard," she said loudly. "I know that it's late in Geneva now, but I assume that you're still up."

"Hey, Ginny, my favorite sister." He laughed. "Don't worry. I say the same thing to Susan when we talk. Yes, I'm up, and next to me is Carmen who, I'm sure, would like a word with you after we finish talking."

"Great. I have some news for you. Maybe it's because of the virus lockdown and because we're all so isolated socially, but I've met a guy in Riverside Park…I actually ran into him on my bicycle a few weeks ago, and we've been talking almost every day in the park and on the phone. Social distance is prevailing….no hugging or kissing. But I sense that this may change. In any case, my boring life as a fledgling lawyer is not so dull right now. This guy is taking a lot of my attention, and I'm happy about that."

"Wonderful, Ginny. Good luck with that. On my side, I'm working from home, but once a week or so, I drive to the Palais, sneak into the office, and spend a few hours there. We're all officially banned from doing this, but most everybody on our team finds a way to go to their office now and then. I see that Carmen is yawning, either because I'm boring her or because it's late. She's also working at her home or mine." He passed the phone to Carmen, and she and Ginny had a brief, affectionate chat. Ginny repeated her wish that Carmen come to the States with Richard for Christmas whatever the virus situation was, and Carmen said that she would row a boat across the Atlantic if flights were still suspended.

The same evening Ginny called her younger sister Susan in Berkeley. They spoke frequently, but Ginny hadn't mentioned Danny in any previous conversations. First she asked Susan about her live-in boyfriend Josh, and Susan said that everything was going well. However, Josh was begging her to come with him to Seattle to visit his family next week, and although she was contemplating it, she hadn't fully decided.

"Sure, I'd like to go and meet his parents, although that could be nervous making. Seattle was the first place on the West Coast to have coronavirus cases, and a number of people died in a nursing home. Seattle is still locked down. If I went, I would have to fly, not a good thing to do these days. So what is your big sisterly advice? Shall I throw caution to the wind or remain housebound in Berkeley?"

"Stay in Berkeley and be vigilant, Suzie. I don't think that it would be a good idea for you to go to two airports and sit in a plane where some people may not be wearing masks. I don't see a compelling reason for you to go right now. If Josh makes a fuss, tell him that your big sister ordered you to stay put in Berkeley for the time being. If he becomes an asshole about it, tell him that I would like to talk with him, and you can be sure that I will kick his butt."

Susan laughed loudly. "Ginny, you're wonderful. My distinguished big sister. I bet that you don't talk like that at your law office."

"No, I don't, but the guys certainly do..or did when we were all at the office. Since I'm for gender equality, I'm going to swear like a sailor when I return to my office. Anyway, my law office is closed indefinitely for now. Now listen up. I have an ulterior motive for calling you…I've met a guy, a guy whom I'm interested in." She told Susan the story of their colliding in Riverside Park and the aftermath up to the present day.

"That's great, Ginny. He sounds special."

"He may be. I'm being my usual cautious self. No kissing or anything else so far. We talk a blue streak every time we meet, and we never seem to run out of subjects to talk about."

"That's fabulous, Ginny. No matter how good things can be in bed, one spends a small time proportionally there with one's partner in comparison to the time spent together outside of bed. My sex life with Josh is still great, but we certainly don't do it every day or every night, and we are together every day and night, and it would be terrible if we had nothing to talk or joke about. Like you guys, we're doing pretty well in the communication area." They said good-bye and vowed to speak again in three or four days.

In addition to telling their siblings, Ginny and Danny also talked to their close friends about each other. Their friends were amazed that each had met someone special during the lockdown crisis. Many of the unattached folks were languishing on dating sites, and it seemed next to impossible to meet someone that way now.

"Fuck," Danny's friend Adam said. "I broke up with Sally just before the lockdown, and I'm busting my balls trying to find somebody cool on three different dating sites. Maybe I'll give it up and head to Central Park, which is closer to my apartment than Riverside Park, and see if I can find a beautiful woman biker to run into me. Or does that only happen in Riverside Park?"

"Go for it Adam," Danny said. "It worked for me. The worst thing that can happen to you is a broken leg."

"Funny man. That's the last thing I need right now. I jog or walk around the reservoir almost every day, but when the weather sucks, I use my stationary bike in my apartment. I would go bonkers locked down at home with a broken leg. On a more positive note, why don't you ask your sultry maiden if she has a female friend for your cool male friend Adam? I'll even take somebody who isn't Jewish, although I'd prefer a Yid like myself."

"Okay, Boychik. I'll check with her on that. I doubt it, but if she does, I'll get back to you right away."

"You didn't tell me if your damsel was Jewish or Christian, Yiddish or Goy. I'm aware that you forgot your Bar Mitzvah of long ago, but, trust me, your Bar Mitzvah has never forgotten you."

"Adam. Ginny's ex-Christian, I believe. I'm waiting to introduce her to my spiritual study of Metapsychiatry. I failed to convert you to that, but maybe she will be susceptible."

"Don't mess around with a goy, my boy."

"Oh, great," said Danny. "Now you're a religious poet. You've got a long way to go on that, you boy toy."

"Utter bullshit from you, as usual," said Adam. "Just don't forget to ask your Ginny if she has a nice friend to introduce to your alter ego."

A few days later, Danny mentioned Adam's request, but Ginny said that her single friends, as far as she knew, were either living with their boyfriends or involved long distance with them.

Ginny's friends were astounded when she told them that she had met by accident (literally) a man in Riverside Park whom she was seeing as a friend now, but with seemingly good prospects that it could develop into something more.

"So interesting, Gin," said her close friend Alissa. "I'm very happy for you." Then she added: "I don't think that I've told you, but I've broken up with Sidney. He went to Maine to stay with his parents, and he was fine for a couple of weeks, but then he went into a funk and became uncommunicative. I told him that I was lonely and that if we couldn't be happy together long distance, we should move on. And, sad to say, his reaction was complete silence."

"Ugh," Ginny said. "That's terrible." Then thinking for a moment, she said: "Alissa, I may have a thought for you. My friend Danny happened to ask me a week ago if I knew a nice woman whom his friend Adam might contact. I've never met Adam, but as Danny's close friend, he's probably a decent guy. And like you, he's Jewish. Shall I pass on your contact information?"

"Hey, it can't hurt. Pass it on."

And Ginny did. And Adam contacted Alissa.

Chapter 6

One day Danny said: "Ginny, I have a suggestion for us. It's not likely, I know, but if our conversation ebbs, if we ran out of things to talk about, why don't we bring our novels to the park to read and maybe even read aloud from them to each other?"

"Great idea. They're both about plagues and so they're unfortunately pretty timely."

Having finished reading 'The Red and the Black', Ginny had now started to read Gabriel Garcia Marquez's masterpiece 'Love in the Time of Cholera' which Danny ironically had read a year earlier. Danny was still reading 'The Plague', enjoying the spare language and unfolding development of characters caught in a vicious plague, although he shuddered at the vivid descriptions of rats and the spreading virus in the Algerian coastal town of Oran. Each day, they found time to read passages from their novels to each other.

"Okay, Ginny. Your turn." Danny said one day after reading a couple of gloomy passages from 'The Plague'.

"What a melancholy scene that was," Ginny said, shuddering. "Dying rats, dying people, horrible atmosphere all over the city. At least Marquez writes lush, romantic scenes. Not all doom and gloom."

Ginny then began to read:

"On the morning of his return from the inconclusive journey, he learned that Fermina Daza was spending her honeymoon in Europe, and his agitated heart took it for granted that she would live there, if not forever then for many years to come. This certainty filled him with his first hope of forgetting. He thought of Rosalba whose memory burned brighter as the other's dimmed. It was during this time that he grew the mustache with the waxed tips that he would keep for the rest of his life and that changed his entire being, and the idea of substituting one love for another carried him along surprising paths. Little by little the fragrance of Fermina Daza became less frequent and less intense, and it remained only in white gardenias."

"Amazing writing, isn't it?" Danny said. "I was entranced last year when I first read it. He's incredibly eloquent. Now I have a wonderful passage for you from another writing of Camus which is certainly relevant to the current plague. Listen to this."

"In the middle of hate, I found there was, within me, an invincible love. In the midst of tears, I found, there was within me, an invincible smile. In the midst of chaos, I found there was, within me, an invincible calm. I realized, through it all, that in the midst of winter, there was, within me, an invincible summer. And that makes me happy, for it says that no matter how hard the world pushes against me, there's something stronger, something better, pushing right back."

"Oh my God," Ginny uttered. "That's so beautiful, so poignant. Whatever is happening, no matter how miserable, he's saying, there is an indomitable spirit within one that can withstand the misery and fight back. A great lesson for our current situation." She was silent for a moment and then said: "The idea of our reading aloud to each other is great. It's such a relief from my work to come here to talk with you and read these passages to each other."

"You still have halfway to go with 'Love in the Time of Cholera,' but I'm almost done with 'The Plague.' Any thoughts on what I should read next?"

"What I would do, and of course I'm not you, is to look again at Camus' 'The Stranger' which I'm sure you read ages ago, but the novel can still be read profitably with its wonderful spare writing and fascinating, almost one-dimensional characters. The novel begins: 'Yesterday my mother died. Or was it the day before. I really don't remember'. Weird, desolate, like the climate of Algiers in the hot summer."

"Mmm," he said. "Let me think about it." When he went home, he immediately ordered 'The Stranger' on Amazon Prime and it arrived two days later.

They spent their time together conversing and reading aloud from 'Love in the Time of Cholera' and "The Stranger.' One day when they finished reading aloud, Danny looked poignantly at her.

"Ginny, I have something to say. I'm feeling really close to you. I cannot recall any communication like this with any other woman I've ever been with. It's really something. What do you think?"

Ginny remained silent for a moment and then said: "Yes, it's the same for me. You and I seem to have great rapport in our communication with each other. I recognize that."

"Yes, and I'll also confess that I'm very attracted to you, and I'm going crazy in not being able to hold your hand or hug you. It's a complete bummer."

"Yes. And I'll confess that I'm attracted to you and wouldn't mind you hugging me right now. Social distancing messes that up, of course, unless we decide to violate it. And I don't know if we should."

"I've been thinking about us and the safety issue. Let's each of us take the antibody test, even though we know that it's supremely flawed. But at least we'll know if one or both of us has had the virus."

"Okay. I'll call my doctor at Mt. Sinai. They're offering the test at $50 a shot."

"Fine. I'll call my guy at Columbia Presbyterian and arrange for it as well.

They both took the antibody test the following week and in both cases, it came out negative.

"Okay," Danny said. "Now we have more information. We know that both of us are clear. It doesn't mean that one or both of us cannot get the virus tomorrow or in a week or a month, but with the sanction of the medical profession, let's carpe diem right now." And he moved closer to Ginny's side of the bench, took her hand, and held it tightly. She tightened her grip as well.

"Ginny, Ginny," he said softly. He hugged her and began to kiss her gently. "This is so nice," he said, as he continued kissing her. He stopped to look into her eyes.

"Danny, Danny, my no longer Invalid…"

"Florence, Florence, my medical and now social savior."

They finally stopped kissing and looked into each other's eyes.

"Marvelous," he said. "I need more of Florence's medicine…"

"Enough 'medicine' for now. My breath is quite taken away…" She pushed him gently from her.

"Mmmm," he said, still holding tightly to her hand, encircling her fingers.

"Maybe we should cool off," she said. "Let's read some Marquez."

"Good idea."

She opened the book and began reading:

"So she had returned. She came back without any reason to repent of the sudden change she had made in her life. On the contary, she had fewer and fewer such reasons, above all after surviving the difficulties of the early years, which were especially admirable in her case, for she had come to her wedding night still trailing clouds of innocence. She had begun to lose them during her journey through Cousin Hilldebranda's province. In Valledupar. She learned at last why the roosters chase the hens, she witnessed the brutal ceremony of the burros, she watched the birth of calves, and she listened to her cousins talking with great naturalness which couples in the family still made love and which ones had stopped, and when, and why, even though they continued to live together."

She looked up from the book a little embarrassed. "I didn't purposely choose that passage, you know."

"A likely story," Danny said, laughing. "Pretty ironic that we were trying to cool down, and lo and behold, you find a sexy passage to keep us stimulated."

She laughed and repeated that it was a 'literary accident'. "Let's stay cooled down for now," she said, taking his hand and holding it tightly.

"Ginny, I cannot believe that after clumsily running into your bicycle a month ago, I find myself on this bench talking a blue streak with you, holding your hand, and now finally kissing you. Truth is truly stranger than fiction."

"Look at you, my highly verbal ex-Invalid. Not only are you an articulate and sexy guy, but you're also becoming a philosopher."

Danny laughed. "Now that we're both clean, I'm going to make an unphilosophical culinary proposal. How about our having dinner together this evening in your apartment? I have a load of prepared food from Citerella, and I will bring it to your table."

She hesitated. Sylvia was supposed to call this evening and engage in sex play with her. She had feigned fatigue the last two times that Sylvia had proposed it. Maybe she should level with Sylvia now and tell her about

Danny. "Okay, ex-Invalid. Let's do it."

An hour later Danny arrived at her apartment with cooked shrimp and red sauce, chicken parmagiana, pasta, and salad, as well as a bottle of Oyster Bay Sauvignon Blanc.

"Hi, guy," Ginny said nervously as she opened the door.

"Hello, Ginny-Florence. Here are the goodies."

"Bring them to the kitchen, please." They walked into her kitchen, and when the food and wine bottle were deposited on the counter, Danny put his arms around Ginny from behind. She leaned back into him holding his arms tightly, and he couldn't help himself from getting an immediate erection. He turned Ginny around, and they hugged, and she could feel the pressure between her legs.

"Danny, Danny, this is new, and I think that we should go slowly. I love kissing and hugging you, but let's take our time doing anything more right now."

"Okay, Ginny. We've entered new territory, and we can certainly take our sweet time, because what we're already doing is very sweet in itself."

"We think alike." They sat on her couch, embracing for a few minutes longer.

Finally he asked: "Wine? Dinner?"

"Wine and cheese first. I shopped at Zabar's and bought some brie and gouda, as well as epoise, a really delicious soft cheese that I discovered in Burgundy a few years ago. Do you know it?"

"I know the first two cheeses, and I'll be happy to experience the unknown epoise. Did I get the French pronunciation right? You spent your junior year in Paris and are fluent in French, but I remember a modicum of

French from my high school days and a couple of courses in college. I've told you that I spent a semester of my junior year at The London School of Economics and Political Science, and I spent the long British academic Easter vacation in Paris. My first time in Paris, and I was entranced, even though it rained almost every day. Fortunately a friend recommended that I take phonetic lessons in order to lose my lousy American accent, and he recommended a French woman teacher who used records and constant repetition to help me sound more French. 'La langue contra les dents,' 'your tongue against your teeth', she said over and over until it hammered into my brain." Danny pronounced the word 'rue' ('street') with a guttural American accent and then an almost perfect French one.

"Yes, I can hear that your accent in French is pretty good in comparison to most Yankees. Maybe if you practice more, you'll be taken for a Canadian from Quebec."

"I'm not sure if that's a compliment. I just wanted to just tell you about my phonetics teacher and her American husband. One evening she invited me to her apartment for dinner, and upon arriving, I met her husband who told me in French that he was from Vermont. When I started to speak English with him, he answered me in French, saying that he never spoke English any more. I asked him why, but he just shrugged and mentioned the Vietnam War, assassinations, and racial turmoil in the States. I remember that it was an uncomfortable evening, but taking phonetic lessons was the best thing I did in Paris that time."

Tasting the epoise on a cracker, he said: "Oh, my. Just terrific. You have good taste in cheese and in men."

"That was a self-serving statement, but I'll accept it."

They drank, ate more cheese, stared into each others eyes, and made desultory conversation.

"It's funny, isn't it?" he said. "Normally we are such parrots, chattering nonstop, and now that I'm in your apartment, our conversation is flagging."

"I'll bet you twenty dollars that we'll rediscover our talkative selves as soon as we sit down to dinner."

"I'm not taking the bet, since I agree with you and since it would be betting against my own interest."

At dinner they slid back easily into conversation, hitting such subjects as their respective junior year college experiences in Paris and London and then discussing their parents and siblings. Danny helped Ginny with the dishes and left about 11 p.m.

Ginny's cell phone had rung twice earlier in the evening and she knew that it was Sylvia. After Danny left, she called Sylvia who was a night owl and would be up until midnight at least.

"Hi, Sylvia. Sorry that I didn't see your calls before."

"Ginny, Ginny. What's up with you? Something is going on…You seem distant. Am I imagining things or am I correct?

"Sylvia, something has happened. You remember my telling you about the guy who ran into my bicycle about a month ago."

"Yeah. I remember asking you if I should be jealous. Since you didn't mention it again, I forgot about him. Has he reared his wounded body and his ugly head recently?"

"You could say so. His name is Danny, and I have been meeting him in Riverside Park hanging out when the weather is good, talking and reading our novels to each other. You're not going to like what I'm going to say, but…a week or so ago, he told me that he really cared for me and asked if we could both take the antibody test to see if either of us had the virus and if so, we would most likely be immune for awhile. So we each took it, and the results came out negative. The test is unreliable, we know, but he took advantage of this to take off his mask and hug me on the park bench today. It's still very innocent, but I am attracted to him and things could escalate between us." She was silent for a moment, as was Sylvia. "I'm really sorry, Sylvia, I know that this must be hurting you…."

"Go on, go on. I'm listening with both ears."

"We agreed to have dinner this evening in my apartment. I bought some cheese, and he brought food and wine. We hugged a bit, but nothing major happened physically between us….We just had a nice time talking at dinner."

"Ginny, I'm hurt. I'm flabbergasted. You've kept this so hidden."

"Nothing was going on with him except friendly conversation, and I thought that we would become friends and nothing more. So I kept quiet about him."

"Nevertheless, you told me twice recently that you were too tired to do pussy time. So I thought that something might be going on." Sylvia hesitated and then asked: "Tell me truthfully, have you slept with him?"

"No, but I think that it might happen in the next few weeks. We've hugged and kissed, but that's all."

"Ginny, Ginny. Maybe you want it both ways. That's difficult, though. I went bisexual for a time when I starting messing around with my roommate at college and still saw men for awhile. Leonard Bernstein did it, as did Georges Sand and some other remarkable women…and men in the Bloomsbury set, for example…But my Ginny…It's not easy to pull off, because both the physicality and the emotionality can get very jangled." She became quiet and then said: "Maybe you're returning to your natural instincts of being attracted only to men. Is he a nice guy, at least? Do you think that he will fuck you over? That is, fuck you and then go on to the next chick?"

"Anything is possible, Syl. He expresses strong feelings for me, and I do like him a lot…But you and I can certainly remain close right now."

"And the pussy time"?

"Not tonight. It's pretty late. But we can hook up tomorrow night, if you like."

"Ginny, you're just saying stuff to please me, not because you really want it." Sylvia went silent for a short time. "I don't think that you intentionally mean it, but all this is very insulting to me. I'm wholly committed to you. I even love you, and now you confess that you've been communicating with a man and will probably sleep with him soon. Where does this leave me"?

"Can't we just be friends for now and see how the situation goes?" Ginny winced because she knew that this idea would hurt Sylvia. But she had to be honest after a month of concealment and deception.

"Friends, schmends. I'm not sure that I can just wipe away the emotional and physical slate between us and pretend that things didn't happen."

"Of course they did. I'm just saying…"

Sylvia interrupted. "It's late now and you've just hit me with a bombshell. I need to think about this. I'll get in touch in a few days."

"Sylvia, Sylvia. I'm so sorry…."

"Ginny, I never should have left you alone in New York. However, the problem may be that you are and have always been a fake fairy. If so, it was my mistake to get involved with you. Good night."

Ginny waited for Sylvia to contact her, but the days went by, and no word came from DC. Ginny sent an affectionate email message to her, but still no reply.

Chapter 7

Life continued with Danny and Ginny as before. They met in the park and sat next to each other schmoozing, reading the NY Times and their novels, hugging in a perfunctory way. They told each other details about the 'significant' others who had been in their lives. Each had had some meaningful, enjoyable relationships, along with some bad ones.

Ginny mentioned a few men whom she had met in college. "Robin, he was a really nice guy. We met in sophomore and were an item until the middle of our junior year. But the ardor cooled, and we stopped seeing each other. Then there was Jeremy, a Jewish wrestler who was also brainy. He was very musical--he had gone to Music and Art High School in New York City, and so we listened frequently to classical music and went to hear the Philadelphia Symphony a number of times. The physical part, however, wasn't so good, and so we decided just to be friends.

"In law school, my first year I went out with a third year student, Steven, and we were together for around a year and a half. Finally the Peruvian artist in the East Village, GianLucca, whom I saw late last year. He gave me an artistic education, taking me to museums, pointing out color patterns, highlighting the differences in the amazing post-Impressionist artists in France in the late 19th century. However, when things were going well--at least I thought they were--he bailed out, saying that I was detached and distant to him and that I had no time for him, given my obsessive need to finish law school. He was undoubtedly right about that. Still, it came as an unpleasant surprise. Since then I've gone out to dinner with a couple of first year lawyers, but no chemistry with either of them. And now that we have the contagion and the stay at home lockdown, I figured that there would be no way that I was going to meet anybody in these conditions. Or so I thought." She smiled at him.

"And what about you, jeune homme? Wait. Before you speak, let me explain that phrase which I've used a couple of times with you. You might think that I'm being pretentious, but there's an historical aspect to it that's pretty interesting. Madam de Pompadour, whose last name was 'Poisson' or 'Fish' in French was the leading mistress of King Louis XV in the mid 1700s. She apparently had a big sex drive, and while walking down the boulevards of Paris or in the Bois de Boulogne, whenever she saw a handsome young man, she would say to him: 'Suivez-moi, jeune homme.' 'Follow me, young man.' And he invariably did, right to her bedchamber, because the handsome young man would be loath to turn down a tryst with the number one mistress of the king. So if I use that phrase with you, take it as my being historically pretentious, not as an invitation to my bedchamber. Okay?"

"Oui, jeune femme."

Ginny laughed loudly. "You do surprise me with your linguistic erudition. So bravo on this one."

"Merci, Ginny," he said, happy that he had one-upped her in French this time.

Ginny looked quizzically at Danny and asked him to tell her about his significant others. "I'm sure that they have been numerous."

Danny looked in the air for a moment and said: "I'm a normal guy. I've always liked women. In high school, college, and even now, I've been lucky in having as many women friends as men friends. I'd like to introduce you to a few of them, but it's obviously not possible during the pandemic. In terms of serious girlfriends, I did the usual dating thing in high school, going out innocently with a few girls in my class or a class or two behind. My libido, however, was at its maximum, and I was pretty frustrated, as all my guy friends were. They say that a man's sex drive is at its peak at age eighteen or twenty, while a women's is strongest in her mid or late thirties."

"I think that's nonsense," Ginny said, "but hey, it gives me something to look forward to."

"Anyway, back to your question…In high school and even junior high school, I secretly lusted after a couple of full breasted babes wearing tight sweaters, but nothing happened. Once I went out with a girl from New York and they always had a reputation for being faster than the girls in Connecticut. So I took her on a car ride, and driving fifty or sixty miles an hour, I put my right hand down her blouse and in her bra in order to feel her breast. She let me do it, and I started to dream that she would let me go further. So I stopped the car on a deserted street, kissed her, and tried to insert my hand into her pants. However, she took a firm grasp of my wrist and put my hand back on her breast. We kissed for a while longer and I then dropped her off where she was staying in West Hartford. I told my close friend Rich about the experience, and he announced to me a week later that he had taken a girl on the Mass Pike and touched her breasts at 70 miles an hour. How pathetic is that? Two lusty young males having a competition in a car as to who could drive more quickly while feeling a girl's boobs. In high school, I enjoyed the studies, the sports, and my friends, but any sexual activity was non-existent. So I remained a virgin until my freshman year in college."

"Funny story. Guys are so different from us complicated, insecure women who feel that we must protect our virginity until the right guy comes along. At least until going to college…"

"You seem the opposite of weak and insecure," he said.

"Maybe so, but I've had my moments of feeling insecure with different guys for a variety of reasons."

"You seem pretty secure in talking with me."

"Yes, I am. Maybe being older and getting to know you pretty well through discussing everything under the sun with you, including the inevitable issue of the opposite sex." She hesitated a moment. "Unless one is a same sex person."

Danny smiled. "I know what you're saying. One of my close friends in college came out a year ago. We're still close friends, of course. As for me, I've never been interested in guys, although I can admire a muscular, strong body and be jealous that I'll never look like that. However, the truth is that I don't want to obsess about weights and hang out in the sun in order to look buff and warrior like."

Ginny was silent for awhile. "I've had a couple of lesbian friends, even one who came on to me. I balked, because it just wasn't my nature. I'm attracted only to the opposite sex, I guess." She had debated in her mind whether to mention her relationship with Sylvia, but she felt that it could rattle Danny, and she didn't want that to take the chance. "So tell me about some of your significant women."

"That's fair. In college I went out with a nice woman from Boston University for a couple of years. I had a car, and I'd drive from Tufts to pick her up in Back Bay, and when the weather was warm, we'd go to the Cape with our books to read and our papers to write and spend the weekend walking on the beach, jumping in the huge ocean waves, studying, and doing you know what."

Ginny smiled. "Sounds pretty nice to me."

"It was. We were together for a couple of years, but our paths diverged when I came to New York for business school and she went to Michigan for graduate work in psychology. We couldn't sustain it, although we have remained friends. Anyway, by that time I had met Claire."

"Who was Claire?"

"My story will not be a pretty picture." He hesitated and then continued. "Believe it or not, we met on the subway at 72nd Street when the local train stalled and we found ourself walking together up Broadway. She was attractive, and I asked for her phone number. Quite soon after we began going out, we experienced a strong romantic attraction, the *coup de foudre,* the thunder bolt, even though I have to confess that the love making was pretty mediocre.

"On our first date, she told me that she was in analysis five days a week. Freudian analysis, the serious stuff. That meant that five times a week she went to see her therapist who raked in almost half of her salary each month. I begged her to cut down, but she was hooked on the analysis and on the shrink whose last name ironically was 'Sunshine'. She wanted me to meet him. So we went together one day, and I could see that he was a charismatic character. But a charlatan as well, because he took me on as a patient after I told Claire I wanted to understand what hold he had on her. She pushed me to talk with him on my own. So I started a five month odyssey seeing her bloody analyst once a week, and all the while it pissed me off that he was violating the customary norms of therapeutic practice by seeing both of us at the same time, and I told him so. He told me that in this case, it was "okay," but I knew that this was bullshit, and it rankled me. Finally, in exasperation and anger, I told him that he was a money hungry bastard, and I quit. I then told Claire to cut down her therapy sessions from five to two or three times a week or I would break up with her. She asked for a month to think about it and make her decision. I gave her two weeks. When the moment came for her to tell me what she had decided, she said that she really needed to see him five times a week. I then said au revoir, but I got pretty depressed about it, and so I began to see a therapist in order to get over her therapist." He laughed. "Complicated, n'est-ce pas?"

"Yeah, it sounds so."

"Have you ever been in therapy?"

"Yes," Ginny replied. "Once, when I was in college…my freshman year. I wasn't happy with my roommate and I was lonely for my parents, and no interesting guy was on the horizon. So I went to the medical clinic and signed up to see a woman therapist."

"How long did it last?"

"I started in early November, and I stayed until the completion of the academic year in late May. I had a good summer living at home working in a day camp, and I felt no need to go back to therapy at the beginning of my sophomore year."

"And since?"

"My sister Suzie in California told me on the phone recently that she had begun to see a therapist, and this gave me an idea that maybe I should also. But the lockdown occurred, and it doesn't seem the moment to begin therapy in a remote way. And I felt fine being at home doing my work and having accidents with runners assaulting my bicycle, although it isn't pleasant being so isolated from family and friends and trying to find ways to ward off boredom."

"Am I an instrument for you to ward off boredom?"

Ginny laughed. "That's a fine way to put it. You keep me entertained, even amused, and that helps me forget any problems that I might have, and you don't even charge any money for your services."

"Maybe I should charge you in kind, in kisses."

"Works for me, jeune homme."

Chapter 8

The next day they met in Riverside Park at noon, Ginny riding her bike and Danny running alongside her on the park sidewalk until 95th Street when she veered off to the left and sped away. He did some calisthenics, looked at the gorgeous flower beds aligning the sidewalk, and sat on a bench awaiting her return. When she reappeared, she slowed down to allow him to run beside her down the hill to 79th Street. She dismounted, and they walked together, he putting his hand on her shoulder.

"This was nice," he said. "Can we do it again soon?"

"Sure. Tomorrow, if you like."

"I like, but I'd better take a day off from running. After the fortuitous accident, my leg is not fully recovered. So how about the day after tomorrow?"

She agreed. He invited her to come to his apartment for dinner that evening. When she appeared, he gave her a tour and then they sat on a couch in the living room next to each other sipping white wine. He leaned over to kiss her. He then put his hand on her breast and opened his eyes to look at her. She had closed her eyes, and he moved his hand inside her bra to feel her right breast. He kissed her passionately and she responded in kind with her tongue. He was now completely turned on, and he told himself that this could be the moment for them to go forward to making love. Moving his hand between her pants legs, he then put her hand on his hard, erect penis.

"Ginny, Ginny….Can we? Can we? Only if you want to…"

She looked at him. "I want to, I want to. I'm just afraid that if we do it now, we may be rushing things. I can be old-fashioned, I know. Am I being crazy as well?"

Danny took a deep breath and took her hand tightly in his. "I think about you when I'm not with you. I'm gaga over you. This is for real. I've never met anyone before now to whom I'm so attracted and happy to be with." He took a deep breath. "It's okay to stop here today. Tomorrow is another day, as Scarlet O'Hara said at the end of 'Gone with the Wind.' Of course she had just rebuffed Rhett Butler, alias Clark Gable, and I'm merely Daniel Miller, a feeble comparison to the sophisticated, devilishly handsome Clark."

Ginny laughed. "In my eyes you're better looking than both Rhett or Clark. Much more my type. So no more invidious comparisons, please. Let's keep talking and save the physical for later or for another day."

"Okay, you clever wench. You've cooled my ardor, and I have retreated into softness and passivity." He looked down at his crotch.

"I bet that you have instant recall when you want to summon him to action," she said, laughing.

"You give me more credit than I deserve. I'm no sexual superman, but with you next to me, anything is possible. For now, though, I'm more like the feeble Clark Kent, not the sexually strong, illustrious Clark Gable." Then he said: "Let's refill our wine glasses and have dinner. Are you fine with that?"

"Yes, very fine. I don't want you to think that I'm not attracted to you and that I'm not torn about this. I want to do…you know what, but just not tonight. Are you sure that you're okay with this?"

"Completely okay. As long as I have you sitting across the table from me and allowing me to gaze into your lovely blue eyes and full lips." He reached out to touch her face.

"You're a charmer," she said, "and also a good cook…or maybe a purchaser of good food." She put her hand on his and said: "I hope that patience is also one of your virtues."

"Ginny, I'll wait for however long it takes for you to feel confident that we're doing the right thing together. Let's drink up this bottle so that I can open another, if we wish." And they did.

A few days later in her apartment it happened.

Ginny had cooked a lamb stew, along with ratatouille, purple-colored small potatoes, salad, and blueberry pie with ice cream for dessert.

Danny brought a bottle of Bordeaux Grave wine into her kitchen. "This looks amazing," he said as she stirred the lamb stew.

"I hope that you'll like it. My mother's recipe from days of yore. The accompanying things are my idea."

"Mmm. Can't wait to sit down for dinner. Can you stop for a minute so that we can have a glass of wine?"

"Yes, young man." She put the cover on the red pot and joined him on the living room couch. He handed her a glass of the wine.

"This is excellent," she said. "We've had this before. Right?

"Yes. Grave from Bordeaux. You liked it a lot, and so I bought a case the next day." He raised his glass. "Here's to you and to us."

"I'll drink to that. To us."

They clinked glasses. After a few minutes Danny moved next to her and kissed her. Looking at her, he took the glass from her hand and put both glasses down on the small table next to the couch.

"I've been thinking about kissing you all day. May I put my idea into practice?"

She nodded. "Works for me. I also thought about it during my dreary work day. It brightened me up and kept my spirit in a happy place. Come here, jeune homme..." She held her arms open and he moved to embrace her.

They kissed passionately, and Ginny became short of breath. She leaned her head back and said: "Maybe now is the time..."

He nodded and lifted her up to hug him. He unbuttoned her shirt and took it off. Unhooking her bra, he put his hands on her nipples and then kissed each of them gently, licking and sucking them.

Ginny shuddered and then said: "Let me," as she unbuttoned his shirt and let it drop on the floor. They hugged each other with their flesh melded together.

Danny undid her pants button, allowing them to slide off. He put his hand inside her panties and felt her soft, moist flesh. Then he put his finger inside her vagina, and she groaned with pleasure.

"Now you," she said, as she undid his outer pants. Soon they were naked in each others arms. She touched his erect penis, applying pressure and rubbing him slowly up and down. His turn to groan excitedly... After passionate kisses and mutual touching, they moved to the bedroom. They hugged and touched and sucked, and finally Danny entered her. He held her back tightly and then put his left hand on her right breast as they moved together sinuously for a long while, softly and then with quicker movement and greater passion. Suddenly he exploded, and she uttered a cry of happiness in response. Gently he came out of her and began to touch her vagina, seeking the spot which he hoped would give her maximum pleasure. After a few minutes she thrust her body forward and shouted cries of pleasure. They lay together without speaking for several minutes looking into each others' eyes.

"I don't know what to say," Danny uttered. "It was phenomenal. Your idea of waiting was brilliant. It built up all my unrelieved passion which exploded in you tonight." He smiled at her while still holding her tightly.

"Me too. I'm not used to this; it's been a long while. But I'm feeling wonderful in all senses with you."

Danny kissed her and said softly: "The first time can be tricky, but our first time went beautifully, I thought."

"Yes, yes," she said, thinking momentarily of Sylvia who hadn't contacted her since that evening of Ginny's revelation about Danny. As she lay peacefully, she thought: 'I'm so happy with this guy. No way that I can go back to my life with Sylvia. Only forward…'

"Penny for your thoughts," he said. "You seemed to be musing about something."

"Just enjoying the moment," Ginny said. "The incredible time we had...are having."

"Ginny, Ginny. I should keep my big mouth shut, but if tonight isn't the time to say it, I don't know when is." He looked a her for a moment and finally said: "I think that I'm in love with you. I don't think it. I know it. I've even told a few friends that I'm in love with Jeanine Reynolds, and they congratulated me."

"Danny, you big left-handed hunk. You really love me?

"Yes, yes, I do. Without a doubt."

"Then I can tell you that I'm also in love with you."

"Are you sure?" he asked quietly.

"Yes, yes. Why would I spend all this time with you, talk with you nonstop, kiss you endlessly, and feel the urge to make love to you, but hold back to await the right moment? Did you think that I was just killing time?"

"You're sure that it's not just the virus situation which isolates us and keeps you away from other men?

"I could ask you the same question. If we weren't locked in our individual compartments, nay, apartments, you would undoubtedly be gallivanting about.. meeting desirable young women, having the pick of the lot."

"No, Ginny. That's nonsense. I feel so lucky that I accidentally ran into your wheels in the park. Look where we are now."

"Same for me, Daniel Miller. We've now crossed the Rubicon. Where do we go from here? To Rome like Caesar?"

"Yes. As soon as the lockdown ends, let's go to Paris and Rome on a trip together. We can make delicious love wherever we go."

"Sounds great. If I knew when that would be, I'd ask for leave time from my firm right now."

"We'll figure it out when we can," Danny said. "I'll ask my boss Daniel Miller for a long leave time with Jeanine Reynolds. I think that he'll agree. Now I suggest that we take a shower and have your delicious stew. Shall we shower together?"

"We can, jeune homme." And they did.

At the dinner table, they ate ravenously, drinking glasses of the Grave wine. Over dessert Danny looked at her and said:

"Ginny, I'm going to look into your eyes and make a small speech. I want to say that I'm very happy with you. You're not only attractive and intelligent, but very caring as a person, from the first moment we met when you stopped your bike and went with me to the clinic. What luck for me to be run into by Jeanine Reynolds on her bicycle, and then spend days and weeks with her in the age of the virus….and now making love with her and holding her luscious body which I suspect I will not be able to get enough of…More importantly, however, is the fact that…" Tears came to his eyes. "I'd better stop here or I will begin wailing from all this emotion."

"Danny, Daniel Miller. You've spoken beautifully. I want to say that this has been a great time for me as well, being with you, talking endlessly with you, and now…making love together. I feel lucky to have found a guy who not only lives two blocks away from me, but also has an excellent sense of humor, super intelligence, and a great body. I've known grouches, known insecure guys who couldn't tolerate even my meagre supply of brainpower, felt threatened by it….But here you show up in my bike path and I run you down and it has led to spending all this time with you. I hope that it continues after the pandemic, but I'll happily take it in the moment now. Unless, Daniel Miller, you've planned this as just a one night stand?"

"You jest, Madame, you jest. We can sign a six month or even a one or two year contract, as Bertrand Russell proposed that beginning couples do. To be renewed upon termination, if both agree. You're a lawyer, so you can draw it up."

"I will be happy to do so if this will make you more secure," she said.

"Ginny, I'm joking. Now that we've found each other, no time limits apply. At least that's how I'm thinking. I want a long period of mutual exploration together, not only in bed, but wherever it leads us. To Paris and Rome after the lockdown ends, but for now on the upper West Side of New York City."

"In Paris we'll have fabulous croissants at breakfast and fantastic meals at some of my favorites restaurants."

"And I'll take you for the most delicious gelato and pasta places in Rome. Let's book our flights now."

Chapter 9

A week later Ginny received the following message from Sylvia. "I've moved on. New person. Same sex."

Ginny waited a day and then sent the following reply: "Happy to hear your news. I'm still involved. Same person. Opposite sex."

Chapter 10

The virus lockdown lasted until December 1, 2020 when Governor Cuomo announced a partial reopening of New York City. Slowly things gravitated to the new "normal" of mask wearing and social distancing on busses and subways, in restaurants, and in offices. Danny returned to his office in February 2021, while Ginny was summoned back to her law office in April. In November 2020 they had decided to live together, each negotiating with his/her former roommate which apartment to abandon and which the two would take over. Ginny's roommate had decided to stay in Vermont and buy into a health food store, while Danny's roommate wanted to return to their apartment at the beginning of the new year. So Danny moved into Ginny's apartment in mid-January 2021. He had his own bedroom where he stored his clothes and set up a desk to read and work.

"You have this great big bed," Ginny said one evening, "and you're crashing in my room. While it's delightful, I'm thinking of kicking you out of my bed when you snore loudly and banish you to your own room."

"Fat chance," he said. "Try it at your peril." And he wrestled her down on her bed and kept her pinned until she said: "Uncle Danny," and he let her go. She promptly jumped on him, pinning his arms, and he said: "Aunt Ginny."

Their life together had multiple aspects. Each continued to work diligently. Danny's firm got more clients, and a large technical firm in Palo Alto began to negotiate with him and his partners about buying them out. Weeks of discussions and negotiations ensued, initially among the three partners, then with lawyers and finally with the California group. It took months to iron out the contracts, and when things looked grim, the California company came through with a financially suitable offer, as well as the provision that two of the principals and all three of the underlings could remain with the company for a period of at least two years. One of

Danny's partners was happy to bail out with over five million dollars in his bank account and move to Boulder, Colorado to watch college football and basketball games, run up and down the steep hills, compose music, and play his guitar in a small band. Danny as president and chief officer was given seven million dollars in the buyout.

"What shall I do, babe?" he asked Ginny one evening at dinner. "I can stay or I can agree to leave with an extra half million dollars to accompany me. I liked being the boss of the former company; now I'll be number three, but with a fair bit of autonomy, a nice salary, and the seven million dollar payoff. If I leave, I don't know what I'll do in terms of work. There won't be any financial pressure, but I'll need to do something. I can't hang around and be a lazy bum. I think that you know this much about me."

"Sometimes one can talk about the lesser of two evils," Ginny replied. "You now have to choose between the greater of two goods. You are in a problematic, but envious position. If you stay for one or two years, you will have stability. If you leave and you don't know what you will do or how you will spend your time, it could be psychologically unsettling. You know that I work long and often intensive hours. I would be a little afraid that in this little couple which we have formed, there will be a major inequality and disparity in the allocation of time and in our individual involvements in the relationship. I'll give you an example. Let's say that you want to do some major traveling, say for a quarter or even half the year. Well, there is no way that I could go with you. And I'm not letting you wander around Paris and Rome sending off endorphins that entice all the young beauties to come close to sniff your delicious scent and admire your curly blond locks and ultra masculine body."

Danny laughed loudly. "An enticing thought the way you put it, but no way. We're getting settled together and I ain't gonna jeopardize that." After thinking for a moment, he said: "You make an excellent point about the difference in career and time involvements we would have. I cannot keep up with you in terms of the hours you work, and I hope that one day you will be able to cut down. But I know that you cannot do that now.

"So, fuck it, I'm going to accept the two year offer, and if it becomes unbearable, I'll leave after a year and find something else to do. Hey, I know the work well, and I enjoy developing the technology and marketing it. What I don't know and can't predict is how I'll get on with the two principals who will be above me, the new president and vice-president. They seem to be nice people, both the man and the woman. But business is business, and you never know. They may want to assert their power quickly and not brook any opposition from the guy who started the company and made it a relative success, but now cannot let go and is clinging to it by his fingernails."

"Danny, it's true that it could be complicated. With human relations, there is no sure way to predict or meld them to your desires and needs. However, if you stay a year, you'll be well paid, have reasonable autonomy, as you've described it, and if it becomes unbearable, you probably could negotiate a termination date earlier than a year. They may pay you well to get you the hell out of there."

Danny got up to kiss and hug her. "Damn, you're a smart cookie. If necessary, I will recruit you to negotiate for me. The fee will be paid in kind. Are you okay with that?"

"Yes, smart ass. Does that mean that you are strongly considering accepting to stay for one year and maybe two?"

"Yeah, I guess so."

Now she got up and kissed him. "Good move, jeune homme. We've just begun living together and we don't want to mess it up. If I'm working endless hours and you are moping around the apartment or reading in Riverside Park on your solitary bench, that would smell like trouble."

"No worries, Ginny. You've convinced me. I'll stay with the new company for at least a year, and if things go reasonably well, for two. I'll sniff around on the outside as well. As President Dwight D. Eisenhower once said: 'The future lies ahead'."

"Wonderful, young man. I raise my glass to toast you and salute your wise decision."

They clinked glasses and sipped their favorite red wine.

Chapter 11

Danny and Ginny resumed social life with their respective friends, individually and as a couple. They also decided that it was important for each of them to meet the other's parents. So one weekend they drove to West Hartford for Ginny to meet Danny's parents, and the following weekend to New Rochelle for Danny to meet her parents. They deemed the visits a success, even though each mother expressed some small reservations about the partner of her daughter or her son.

"Mothers will be mothers," said Ginny after the two visits. "No one is good enough for their daughter or their son. So no sense getting into a stew about their petty complaints. Okay?" Danny just shook his head in mild exasperation.

Each of Ginny's friends wanted to meet Danny and his friends, Ginny. So they decided to give a party in their apartment shortly after the reopening of New York life, requesting that all of their guests be double vaccinated, as they were. The event was a big success socially, gastronomically (they used a Moroccan caterer), and alcoholically, with Danny ordering two cases of Grave Bordeaux wine from the liquor store on West 79th Street, the only place in NYC that carried it, along with New Zealand Monkey Bay and Oyster Bay dry Sauvignon Blanc. The party was a raucous, jolly affair, with Ginny meeting Danny's men friends and he meeting her women friends for the first time. Everyone congratulated them on their ingenuity of beginning a relationship during the lockdown era of the coronavirus.

"Amazing story," Ginny's friend Emily said. "Inspirational even."

Danny's close friend Adam came to the party with Ginny's intimate friend and law school classmate, Alissa, thanks to Adam asking Danny during the lockdown to see if Ginny knew a nice woman to introduce to him.

"We're an item," Adam whispered to Danny, "and we owe it all to you guys."

"Yeah, Adam. Alissa is one of Ginny's best friends, and she's delighted that we could match you two. However, on my side, I'm convinced that I have ruined Alissa's life."

Adam laughed and punched Danny's arm lightly. "Motherfucker. Good thing that I opened my big mouth to you about you asking Ginny if she knew anyone for me to meet after my break-up with Sally, and lo and behold, it worked like a charm. You produced Alissa, and she's even Jewish and we've gone to synagogue together. You guys should go into the marriage counseling business, especially during pandemic lockdowns."

"What a bad idea. As if Ginny and I have abundant time to dabble in the fix-up field. She works like a dog for her law firm, and I'm trying to negotiate a buy-out of my small tech firm. But you guys could undertake it, and we'll provide crucial support. You can name your new business: 'Truth is Stranger Than Fiction', and you can cite the story of how Ginny and I met in Riverside Park, with me accidentally crashing into her bike during my run."

"Danny boy, you've told me the story several times, but it sounds fishy, even suspicious. Are you sure that you didn't plan it all?"

"Are you nuts, Adam? Don't be an asshole. Yeah, I spent hours and days figuring out how to meet this damsel on her bicycle and decided to run into her bike. That's hocus pokus, and you know it."

Adam winked at him. "You're a clever cat, my boy, and nothing that you do would surprise me. One day you'll confess to me that I figured you out. I can wait patiently for that, since your crash meeting has produced Alissa in my life."

"Let's talk to Ginny now, since she's eager to check out your 'ugly face', as Alissa has described it."

"Bastard. I'll get you for that," Adam whispered in Danny's ear as he led them to the other side of the room where Ginny was surrounded by a crowd of noisy friends, including Alissa, Nancy, and Theo, the three who had gone to Europe with her the previous summer. The two guys waited patiently until Ginny and Alissa broke away to come to them.

"The second best thing that has come out of Danny and my meeting," Ginny said, putting her arms around Adam and Alissa.

Alissa smiled, and Adam held up his wine glass and said: "I'll drink to that."

"Next weekend, Saturday," said Danny. "Let's the four of us go out for dinner."

And they did.

Chapter 12

The following Saturday they made plans to meet in the West Village for dinner at a Spanish restaurant serving superb sangria and overflowing platters of delicious paella. Danny and Ginny decided to go to the Whitney Museum in the mid-afternoon beforehand. They had each been there individually, but this was their first time as a couple.

The museum, as usual, was packed with people. They started on the third floor looking at wild modern art paintings and sculptures, working their way towards the stairs to walk down to see the Hoppers.

Suddenly Ginny saw Sylvia and another woman walking in their direction.

"Sylvia," Ginny said, hugging her briefly. "How great to see you. I guess that you're back in New York now."

"Yes, that's right. I came back a month ago. Oh, let me introduce you to Kim."

Ginny and Kim shook hands. Ginny then introduced Danny to the two women.

"Very nice to meet you, Danny," said Sylvia, smiling broadly.

"Same for me," Danny said.

Kim smiled, but remained silent.

"We're meeting some people for dinner," Ginny said. "But let's think about getting together some time soon."

"Yes, of course," Sylvia said. "Again, nice to meet you, Danny."

As the two couples walked in different directions, Ginny looked back, and she saw Sylvia put her arm around Kim's waist, raise her thumb, and wink at Ginny.

"Who were they, Sweetie?" Danny asked.

"An old friend who teaches at NYU. I haven't seen her in months because of the lockdown. She went to DC to be with her parents, and it's nice that she has returned to resume her life in the Big Apple."

"Kim looked sort of butch," Danny said. "Do you agree?"

"I didn't really study her. So I can't comment on that. Let's go to the second floor to see some great art before we have to leave to meet Adam and Alissa."

"Fine idea."

Chapter 13

In May 2021 they took their long awaited trip to Paris and Rome. With Ginny leading the way in Paris, they wandered along the Seine, scrutinized the damage done by the raging fire at Notre Dame Cathedral two years earlier, sat on chairs in the Luxembourg Gardens, made a foray to Montmartre, ate magnificently in French, Algerian, and Vietnamese restaurants, went to several museums including the Louvre, the Musee d'Orsay, and Musee du Quai Branly, made a visit to the Arab Center in Paris, took a day trip to Chartres to see the magnificent cathedral, and made love almost every day in a small hotel on the Left Bank overlooking the Seine and Notre Dame that Ginny had arranged for them.

"Amazing city," said Danny. "I'm certainly looking at it with new eyes. I realize how much I don't know. You could be a tour guide here."

"I'm just improvising," Ginny said. I spent a full year at the Sorbonne, and I've returned five or six times since. So if I don't know Paris, I know nowhere."

"Your modesty is underwhelming," he said.

"Wise ass," she said, pushing him down on the bed.

Ginny's brother, Richard, and his girlfriend, Carmen, drove to Paris from Geneva to have a magnificent lunch with them at the elegant restaurant La Cascade in the Bois de Boulogne, with Danny happily footing the outrageously expensive bill. Conversation flowed easily, with Richard and Danny enjoying each other's company and making quips about life in overcharged New York versus life in sleepy Geneva.

"He's great," Richard whispered to Ginny when they said good-bye. "Hold on tightly to him." Ginny smiled and shook her head affirmatively.

They flew to Rome where Danny took the lead, since he knew the city well, having been there a number of times. He had booked a fancy hotel near the Spanish Steps, and he planned walks to the Forum, the Piazza Navona, the synagogue in the Jewish ghetto and older districts like Trastevere where he arranged meals in small restaurants that he either knew from past trips or looked up on Google. Danny arranged a couple of fancy meals at the elegant restaurants Del Sostegna and Cul de Sac (Ginny appreciating the French name of that wine bar featuring smallish plates of delicious food). Since both were concerned about consuming an overload of pasta and putting on some serious extra weight, they justified their daily intake of delicious pasta by walking for several hours each day. Danny even did his push-ups every day on a sidewalk next to the Tevere River.

Two days before their departure, Danny took Ginny to the Colosseum where she had been once before, but remembered very little. Briefing himself before the trip, Danny impressed Ginny with his abundant knowledge of ancient history, citing statesmen and emperors going back to the Roman Republic and the Roman Empire. He even talked knowledgeably about Mussolini and the rise of fascism in the early 1920s, well before the advent of Hitler and Nazi Germany.

"You're quite an authority on this magnificent ruin, as well as on Italian history," Ginny said in the Colosseum after he had related fascinating historical events to her for almost an hour. "I'm very impressed with your historical knowledge."

"That's nice to hear," Danny said, "but now I am going to try to impress you even more."

"What do you mean?" asked Ginny.

Danny led her to a quiet deserted spot off to the side. Clasping her shoulders, he pushed her down gently onto a large ancient rock. He then got down on his knees.

Before he could speak, Ginny said quickly: "Oh, my God. Is this what I think it is?"

"Jeanine Ginny Reynolds: 'Je t'aime. 'Te amo'. I love you. I love everything about you. I want you to be with me for the rest of our lives. Will you marry me?" He took a small box from his pocket. It was an engagement ring.

"Danny, Danny. Are you sure? Are you absolutely sure?"

He kept his serious expression and nodded. "Yes. I've been thinking about this for months. I almost did it in New York, but I knew that this would be more memorable."

"In that case, jeune homme, I most happily and lovingly accept your marriage proposal." She lifted him gently up, and they hugged for a long time.

"The ring," she said. "I think that it goes somewhere on my hand."

"Of course," he said, sliding the ring onto her fourth finger. "It should fit well, because I smuggled a couple of your rings to take to the jeweler in order to get your right size. You'll have to go to the jeweler--we'll go together--to make it fit perfectly on your finger. By the way, this diamond is from my mother's engagement ring. When I told her a few weeks ago that I was going to propose to you and that I was intending to buy a diamond, she stopped me cold and said that she wanted to give her diamond to me for your ring."

Ginny teared up and said: "That is so great. Can we call her so that I can thank her?"

"Of course. We're going to call everybody--my parents, your parents, Joel, Susan, Richard. I think that they'll all be very happy for us."

"Not as ecstatically happy as I am right now." She held her finger out and gazed at the ring. "It's so beautiful. Come here, you big hunk, and let me hug you more."

They embraced for what seemed like an eternity. A few tourists who had witnessed the event clapped and shouted: "Bravo, bravo, felicitations…"

"Merci, merci" Ginny shouted back. Danny smiled and waved at them.

Danny then looked at her with a solemn expression on his face. "Ginny, now I am going to reveal a secret to you. Nobody else knows, but I think that you should know, and I want to tell you."

"What the heck do you mean? Are you gay? Are you going to join the Marines and go to Afghanistan? Do you secretly work for the C.I.A.? Are you about to die? What can be so important to tell me after you propose marriage and I accept?"

"I don't know if I should even open my big mouth about this, because maybe you will balk. Maybe you will hate my guts. I don't think so, but.. who knows?"

"Spill it out, please. You're driving me crazy. Is it a very bad thing?"

Danny smiled: "No, it's a very good thing."

"Okay, spill the beans. Now, immediately..I insist." Ginny looked at him with a solemn expression.

"Ginny, do you remember how we met?"

"Of course. I'll never forget it. I ran into you on my bike in the park."

"No, that's not accurate. I ran into you. I planned in advance to run into your bicycle because I couldn't figure out any other way to meet you. And I wanted very badly to meet you?"

"What are you saying?"

"I had seen you a few times in Riverside Park sitting stationary on your bike without your helmet on. You were fixing your hair, and I was very attracted to you. Maybe it was partially the pandemic lockdown, but I found myself thinking about you a lot, and I racked my brains trying to figure out a way to meet you. There was one opportunity that I tried to take advantage of, but you left too quickly."

"What do you mean?"

"Do you remember the day when you were riding and I was running and it began to storm?"

"Yes, vaguely."

"It stormed vigorously, and a number of people hurried to the playground house around 82nd Street. There were maybe ten or twelve of us there. We were both standing around waiting for the rain to end. I was about to make an inane comment about the weather to you when the rain suddenly ended, and before I could say anything, you got on your bicycle and rode quickly off. That convinced me that I had to come up with a plan to meet you."

"I think that I am catching your drift," she said.

"The only effective plan that I could think of was to run into your bicycle, fall over, and see if you would stop to comfort me or just ride off. But you stopped immediately and came to my assistance."

"You fell to the ground. Your knee was bloody. Was that a fake as well?"

"No, of course not. I fell down hard, partly on my own volition, and my knee got bloody and did hurt a bit. However, I exaggerated how serious the injury was so that you wouldn't ride off. You immediately sympathized with me and helped me get to the CityMD. The doctor thought that I was crazy when I told him what I had done. I made him swear to secrecy beforehand. So one individual in the world other than us knows my secret, but I'm sure that he has forgotten about it by now."

"And I thought that it was my fault for running into you. And I felt very guilty, as I recall. And now on our engagement day, you're telling me that you secretly and fraudulently arranged an accident in order to meet me. That's pretty brazen, isn't it?"

"It worked, Babe. It worked. We met and got on super well. Do you recall our history as vividly as I do? You walked me home. I bought flowers for you the next day. You thanked me in a text, and this gave me an opening to ask you to meet me on a bench in Riverside Park. You did. The rest is history."

"You faker. I don't know what to say. I'm shocked."

He took her hand between his two. "Look at what has happened as a result of my deciding to run into your bicycle. My little scheme led to a wonderful relationship, and today you have agreed to marry me. I assume that my confession will not induce you to change your mind."

"You schemer. You bloody liar," she said laughing. "I'm stunned, but I'm also impressed with your ingenuity, and I'm not going anywhere except into your arms." She hugged him tightly and then asked: "No one else knows except that doctor?"

"No one. Adam came close to guessing, but I denied it. I think that our families and friends would be fine with the knowledge, but I would prefer to keep it between us. Unless you feel differently."

"No. I agree that it should remain our secret, an essential part of our new conjugal conspiracy. I had some dire thoughts when you began your great revelation. Do you want to know what they were?"

He nodded.

"Some thoughts that flashed through my mind were that you were going to announce that you were gay or bisexual, that you had only a couple of years more to live, that you were a secret C.I.A. or Russian spy, or or that you were going to abandon New York City and move to Bali or New Caledonia. So your great revelation comes as a big relief, even though I should probably be pissed off at you. But how can I be when you've just proposed to me and I've accepted? I wouldn't have suspected in a million years that you crashed into me in the park as the only way to meet me. I suppose that after we met, you planned every step of the way, including when we would go to bed?"

"No, never. I only planned a method of meeting you. I didn't know if you would bike away after our collision, and I certainly didn't know what what kind of person you were." He took her hand and held tightly on her new engagement ring. "The amazing thing is that the results could not have come out better. You are the love of my life, and now you have consented to become my wife. Unless, of course, you want to retract in the aftermath of my little revelation. This is your last chance to do so."

"Fat chance, Daniel Miller. Come back into my arms and hug me tightly now and forever."

Chapter 14

When they returned to NYC, they resumed their work lives and their social and cultural distractions. They luxuriated in discussions about their marriage to take place the following May. However, in August Ginny announced to him that she was pregnant.

"My gynecologist suggested that I change birth control pills and I did. But I may have omitted taking them for a day or two in the transition. Are you happy or upset?"

Danny looked at her with tears in his eyes. "I'm delighted. I've always wanted to be a father and now I will. Damn..it's great. How many months pregnant are you?

"Just three. We'd better wait while to make sure before telling anyone." She held his hand tightly. "I was a little apprehensive, but I knew that you'd come through for me in my newfound pregnancy."

"Sweetie, of course. What did you expect I'd say or do? Don't answer that. I am truly the happiest of men."

"It will mean a big change of life for both of us, as you know. Lots for us to talk about."

"I saw my brother go through it, as well as a few male friends. Now it's my turn. On Sam's frig, as you may have seen, there is a do-dad affixed to it that says: 'Insanity is hereditary. It comes with children'. We'll see about that."

"Not very funny, I'd say. Let's get back to basic issues. I've told only one person, Alissa, and she was excited and comforting. She thinks that our apartment is too small, though."

"I agree. What I would like us to do is to buy a large coop or condo on West End Avenue or Riverside Drive. We are so privileged in not having money problems, thanks to the company buyout and to my and your very decent salaries. I'm willing to take two million from my package and pay off on a big apartment, say, four bedrooms, and then we'll have great space in case another baby comes in the not too distant future. The apartment will be in both our names, of course." Then he looked at her. "We don't want to go to the suburbs, do we?"

"I'm more than happy to stay in the city, particularly in a bigger place. Going to a suburb would save money for education, but we would have hours to suffer the commute both directions for work five days a week. And most all of our friends are in the city. So no suburbs for now. Maybe we could discuss having a weekend place in Connecticut or in the Hamptons. We'd have to decide between country or beach. Both sound appealing. However, please don't rush me into another child. Let's have a couple of years alone with the first one."

"Yes, darling. My mind and imagination have been soaring away since you told me you were pregnant. I'm so happy about your news that I'm projecting far in the future. I promise to stop doing that,"

She hugged him and said: "You can project as much as you want, since it's all good stuff. I feel fine now in the early stage of pregnancy, but in two or three months, my body will change and it could be uncomfortable."

"Right. Of course. One question: have you thought about telling people in your office? How are they with pregnancies?"

"Pretty good. A few women have undergone pregnancies in the last few years, and I've inquired what it was like for them. Two said that the firm was really great in terms of allocation of time at home and working at home for the first six months after birth, and one said that the firm was okay, but could have been better. Naturally I'm going to wait for awhile to be sure that things move ahead well before spilling the beans about my pregnancy. You and I should also have an agreed timetable for telling our families."

"I'd like to tell them right now, but I'll keep my trap shut. Wow. I guess that you are too young to try to find out what gender we will have."

'I'm fine with the uncertainty, but if it bugs you, I could undergo amniosynthesis which will show what gender is in there."

"No, it's fine. I'll be happy, overjoyed, with either gender."

"Good. And we should begin to talk about advancing our marriage date unless we want to walk down the aisle wheeling or carrying a screaming baby. That would indicate to everyone that we had sex before marriage."

Danny laughed uproariously. "Nice thought. Lustful us waiting for marriage before climbing into each other's pants. Very unlikely that anyone will believe that we're asexual and abstemious."

"Yeah. But it does raise the issue about our getting hitched before next May."

"Right. Let's consider what we should do."

They advanced their wedding date to November. It was a jolly affair with over 200 people attending the preliminary events and the wedding, including their siblings, relatives, friends, and significant others. Ginny's brother Richard and his girl friend Carmen came from Geneva, Ginny's sister Susan and her boy friend Josh from California. Everybody on both sides descended to the Boat Basin in Central Park where the ceremony and post-nuptial feast took place. At one moment, Adam and Alissa, each having roles in the marriage ceremony, took the newly married couple aside to inform them that they had gotten engaged a few days before

"A mitzvah, a mitzvah that you guys performed in introducing us," Adam said to the newlyweds. "If you hadn't, we would have met here today, but who knows what our significant other situation would have been and how we would have reacted to each other? I'm convinced that I would have made a beeline in Alissa's direction, but that's easy to say and impossible to prove."

"Great. Great," Danny and Ginny said almost simultaneously to the two of them. Danny whispered: "Don't fuck it up, Adam, or I'll kick your ass." Adam took up a boxing stance and laughed loudly. "Check out my muscles, Danny," as he flexed his right arm. "You would have a bad time of it." They hugged each other and then went for some champagne.

Danny and Ginny went on a boat tour of the Caribbean for their honeymoon. When they returned to New York City, they began looking in earnest for a larger apartment in which to live. After a few months they agreed to buy a four bedroom coop apartment on West End Avenue and 82nd Street.

"Zabars, here we come," said Danny.

"Sweetie, I'm fat now because of the baby. You're a little chubby because of excessive food intake. I think that you should begin a little diet and take off five to seven pounds. That shouldn't be difficult. And in the meantime until you shed that weight, we will boycott Zabar's. Your reward for the weight loss will be a feast of lox and cream cheese, herring, and other goodies. But the scale must prove that you deserve the food intake which I will buy for you."

"Wow," said Danny. "I would not like to be on the other side of a law case against you. You are tenacious, even a bit ferocious…So you think that I am a fat slob now? Okay, I take seriously what you said, and I will begin a diet tout de suite. Plus an increase in exercise. Give me two months and you will lust for my body again, even if your big pregnant belly doesn't feel like welcoming me inside."

"You're a sweetie, my sweetheart. I thought that you might fight me on what I just said, but you took it amazingly well. A mature man you are. Now come here and hug me."

Chapter 15

Ginny and Danny continued to see their friends Alissa and Adam whose marriage would take place a few months after the arrival of the baby. Adam and Alissa moved into a large coop apartment on Riverside Drive and 84th Street close to Danny and Ginny. Adam, an investment banker, and Ginny, a fledgling lawyer, had substantial assets, as well as hefty salaries, to indulge their needs and whims, including the planning of a monthlong honeymoon trip to China, Thailand, and Japan. One Saturday afternoon before Danny and Ginny were going to meet Adam and Alissa for dinner in Lincoln Center, Danny sat Ginny down and said the following:

"Sweetheart. I think that we should reveal to Adam and Alissa how we met in Riverside Park."

"Really?" Ginny uttered. "I thought that we had agreed to keep it our secret."

"Yes, we did agree on that, and we have kept our traps shut on the matter so far. However, they are our closest friends, individually and as a couple, and their involvement and upcoming marriage is directly due to our unorthodox meeting, that is, my running into your bicycle wheel and falling down hard to gain your sympathy...Adam guessed that there was some skullduggery, but I always pooh poohed the matter and told him that he was full of shit. So it may not be a full surprise to him. But that's okay. What do you think?"

"Okay. We can tell them, but ask them to maintain secrecy on the matter."

"Definitely."

Three hours later, the two couples were sitting in a booth at the elegant Chinese restaurant Shun Lee West in Lincoln Center, recently reopened after a year of closure.

Sipping his cocktail, Danny suddenly said: "Okay, guys. Listen up. Ginny and I have an announcement, actually reveal a secret…"

"What the fuck?" said Adam. "We know that you're married and that Ginny is pregnant. Are you going to tell us that Ginny is a lesbian and you're a gay guy and that you are exploring new territory in your marriage of convenience?"

Ginny cracked up laughing. "No, Adam. Nothing so dire. A piece of positive information."

"Go ahead, darling," Danny said. "You tell them."

"Okay. But first, you guys must pledge that you will keep our secret."

"Yes, yes. We pledge," said Alissa after Adam.

Ginny began. "Okay. Here's the scoop. I always figured that Danny accidentally ran into my bicycle in Riverside Park"…

"Adam chimed in. "Oh, shit. I can guess what's coming. Do you remember, Danny, that I was skeptical about your story of an accident?"

"Yup," Danny said. "You are a suspicious, bright pain in the ass. And now we will validate your suspicious nature. Continue, please, Ginny."

"Well, just after Danny proposed to me in the Roman Colosseum and I accepted, he said that he had a deep, dark secret to reveal to me. I figured that he was gay or a CIA agent or had six months to live. However, Danny wanted to reveal to me the actual circumstances of our bicycle accident. He started by confessing that he had seen me a number of times in Riverside Park on my bike, and he had desperately wanted to meet me."

Nodding in affirmation, Danny leaned over to plant a kiss on

Ginny's cheek.

"That was nice. To continue…He said that the only way he could think of meeting me was to crash into my bicycle and hope that I would get off and comfort him. And he did that, drawing blood on his knee and prompting me to get off my bicycle and try to comfort this clumsy oaf who had run into my bike and was now writhing on the ground with blood oozing from his knee. What was I to do? Say that I was sorry and just ride off? No. I got off my bike and offered to help him."

Danny then intervened. "That was what I desperately wanted. It was a gamble on my part. This was the only method that I could think of to meet this comely lass. Don't forget. It was the early stages of the covid period. I was locked down working many hours a day, seeing no one among my friends and family, zooming with my colleagues, bored out of my skull, running in the park for exercise and diversion and then seeing this beautiful creature (Danny put his hand on hers.) a good few times and racking my brains on how to meet her. The only thing that I could come up with as a sure method was to run into her bicycle deliberately, hoping that she would be sympathetic, comfort me, and allow me to get to know her, and best of all worlds, give me her contact information."

"Amazing," said Alissa. "It worked like clockwork. Ginny, the kindest of souls, did stop and even walked you to a CityMD office, if I'm not mistaken. But jumping ahead, isn't it true that we two couples owe our relationships and marriages (you guys already, we in a couple of months) to Danny's reckless, but brilliant idea?"

"Thanks, Alissa," Danny said. "You've got it right. That's why we are telling you our little secret today."

Ginny chimed in. "Danny told me after his marriage proposal that he wanted to begin our new lives on a footing of truth." Looking at Danny, she continued: "The bum even gave me an 'out', saying that if I wanted to cancel my agreement to marry him, this was my last chance."

Danny smiled. "I was terrified that she might do that, but I was also pretty confident that she wouldn't. If she had balked or said that she wouldn't marry me, I would have looked for a Roman sword in a dungeon of the Colosseum and run it through my stomach or heart."

"You shocked me with your revelation, you creep," Ginny said, "but I was then and remain madly in love with you, and your declaration was mild compared to some of the thoughts I had when you said that you had a secret to reveal to me. I thought that maybe he was going to die in a couple of months and therefore wanted to hurry our marriage. My mind soared with dire possibilities. But he explained the incredibly positive benefit of his rash action, his chutzpah, in running into me in Riverside Park. We were now engaged to be married, and so his little scheme has turned into the prospect, nay certainty, of marital bliss for us and now for you two."

Danny chimed in. "Ginny and I made a pact which she called an integral part of our 'conjugal conspiracy', that is, to tell no one what actually happened that day in Riverside Park. However, since a direct result of the so-called accident has been you two guys coming together and soon marrying, Ginny and I feel that you two should know the truth and be our 'partners in crime'."

Alissa was crying, and Adam was teary as well. They came to the other side of the table and hugged Ginny and Danny for a long time.

"We two owe it all to you," Adam said. "So let's be really festive tonight." He asked the waiter to bring the wine list and he ordered an expensive bottle of champagne. When it arrived, he poured four glasses and said: "We thank you, Danny, you creative, silly motherfucker, for planning to run into Ginny's bike and see how she would react. It has led to us two couples engaged in holy, happy matrimony. Here's to Danny and Ginny and to us four. May we all have a magnificent, happy life as married couples and as friends forever." They clinked glasses and uttered affirmations of undying friendship. "And to honor Danny's brilliant move in Riverside Park and to continue on the road to nirvana, I offer, nay, I insist, on paying for tonight's dinner in great gratitude."

"Adam. Did I hear you correctly?" Danny asked. "You're usually a cheap bastard…No, you're not. I just made that up to get back to our routine of reciprocal insults. Thanks, man. We accept and will reciprocate soon." They clinked glasses again.

"One other thing," Adam said. "You guys know about my incredible guitar and voice skills…"

Danny groaned. Turning to Ginny, he said: "This creature opposite us…he thinks that the can play the guitar and sing as well as Paul Simon or Paul McCartney. In reality…."

"Be kind, man," Adam interrupted. "I am going to write and play for you 'The Ballad of Ginny and Danny'." Faking a guitar position with his arms, he sang:

Ginny and Danny, they met in the park.
Their meeting cannot be described as a lark.
The incident was very stark.
Even though he brayed like an aardvark,
His bite was inferior to his bark.
Danny schemed to meet her somehow.
He ran into her bike mooing like a cow.

"Hey guys, I'm just getting warmed up," Adam exclaimed. "Shall I continue?" Just then the food arrived--hot and sour soup; spare ribs, platters of Beijing duck; shrimp with garlic; lamb in hoisin sauce.

"Saved by the arrival of the food," Adam said. "You guys are lucky. I will subject you to further verses when we next meet."

"A shame that Ginny and I are taking a trip around the world," Danny said. They all laughed.

"Hey, man," Danny said. "I liked your lyrics. Please do write more verses and regale us on your guitar when we next see each other."

"You're on, Danny," Adam said, helping himself a large portion of Beijing duck and shrimp and garlic sauce.

Chapter 16

Five years later Danny and Ginny had three children, boy, girl, boy, plus a live-in nanny from Nigeria. Ginny was now a junior partner in her law firm, and she succeeded in convincing the firm to give greater weight to the needs of their female employees. As a married mother, Ginny arranged to have six months off after each birth, and when she returned to her office, she was allowed to spend half of her work time at home. This allowed her to be a nearly full time mother, as well as a close to full time attorney.

On his side, Danny worked hard at the California run firm Allegria Plus for three years before taking six months off to be a full time father of his three small children, taking them to playgrounds in Riverside and Central Parks with Mildred, the nanny, as oten as he could. He was frequently the only male in the playground, and one young mother asked him if he was a male nanny, prompting him to make a bad joke about his name rhyming with the word 'nanny'.

He frequently saw Adam and Alissa's Peruvian nanny who was shepherding their two young children, a boy and a girl, on the swings and slides of the playground at 76th Street. The five children frequently played together in the park, in their apartments, and in the Hamptons. The two couples had each bought a house close to Bridgehampton Beach, and they spent many weekends and a good fraction of the summers hanging out together and arranging play dates with their kids. They vowed to take a vacation in Costa Rica the next January to escape the cold of New York City. Adam even made an appearance once in awhile in Riverside Park, calling Danny in advance to meet him with his children.

One day Danny showed Mildred where he had collided with Ginny on her bicycle, informing her about the 'accident' that had led to their introduction, courtship, and present day marital cum parental status. Mildred said that she was very impressed with the "unorthodox way" Ginny and he had met. As she looked him in the eye, he winked at her. She winked back. "Smart cookie," he said to himself.

After six months of delightful father parenting time, Danny and one of his former partners launched another start-up firm in a highly complicated technical area of robotics which they felt had immense promise.

Danny and Ginny, who met in the preposterous circumstances of a calculated bicycle accident, lived happily ever after.

Postscript

The events depicted in this story are fictitious, the product of the author's imagination and not based on actual people or real events. The story emanates from the context of boredom and solitary confinement induced by the coronavirus lockdown which began in March 2020 and seemed to last indefinitely. For relief and diversion I decided to write a short story which ballooned to over one hundred pages, and so it became a novella.

The aim of the story was to create two primary characters, Danny and Ginny, who were professionally successful, conventional individuals sequestered in their respective apartments on the upper West Side of Manhattan near beautiful, sprawling Riverside Park (close to where I live) and imagine an unorthodox way as to how they might meet (Danny's purposeful collision into Ginny's bicycle). They then began to meet frequently, talk on park benches about their lives and their families, read beautiful passages from pandemic novels to each other, become deeply attracted, and fall in love.

The context of daily life in the pandemic atmosphere of the city has produced misery for so many businesses, for hotels and tourism, for cultural offerings (eliminating live theatre, films, opera, music, etc.), for restaurants, and for education (from primary and secondary schools to colleges). Remote work and remote education became the norm, and this had its advantages and its shortcomings which Danny and Ginny experience and discuss endlessly.

Taking an optimistic approach, I imagined a 'fairy tale' of an accidental meeting (through a contrived 'accident'), followed by the courtship of Danny and Ginny, with growing mutual attraction and deepening emotional and physical intimacy. Frustrated by the covid-induced lack of physical contact, they agree to take the antibody test, and of course they are both negative. This leads slowly to growing physical intimacy, and then rapturous love-making.

Ginny and Danny decide to live together, and when the virus officially 'ends' in January 2021 (remember, this is a fairy tale), they take their long-awaited trip to Paris and Rome. In the Colosseum Danny proposes to a surprised Ginny who naturally accepts. Then he reveals to her his tactical ploy of deliberately running into her bicycle in order to meet her. She is shocked by his revelation, but delighted with its outcome.

Back in New York City, Ginny becomes pregnant, and they decide to accelerate their wedding date. They are both financially successful, allowing them to buy a big apartment on the upper West Side and choosing the lifestyle they wish, leading to the gradual appearance of three children. Danny takes six months off to be a hands-on father in the playgrounds of Riverside Park. In this story, their lives are basically problem-free, a fairy tale fantasy of love spawned in the covid era which will deepen and continue for the rest of their lives.

Because of the political context of the country and its impact upon New York City, the author imagined two characters sharing similar political views, because otherwise they would not have been compatible. Sitting in my study working on the novel, I was drenched by the daily inundation of negative news about the virus engendered by President Trump's dismissal of the severity of the covid issue which has led to well over 500,000 deaths in the country. Danny and Ginny were aghast and angry at the president's machinations and lies, and it seemed to be poetic justice that the president himself should come down with the coronavirus because of his opposition to the notion of wearing masks and taking other elementary precautions against the virus. The presidential election is taking place today (November 3, 2020), and Danny and Ginny have made plans with Adam and Alissa to watch it with several of their friends to cheer on the Democrats to triumph and put an end to these unbearable, divisive four years of Republican rule.

Acknowledgements

I thank a number of friends for their perusal and critical reading of "Love in the Age of Coronavirus." I am grateful for their comments and suggestions re the novella.

I would like to thank my close friend and tennis partner, Bob Salpeter, for offering his marvelous design skills and excellent judgment in proposing a design for the cover and the interior of the novel, as he did in designing the cover and interior of my novel "Diplomacy and Death at the U.N."